A SINGLE SPARK

The Spark Brothers Series Book 1

LIWEN Y. HO

D1607499

A Single Spark

ISBN: 9781706592389

This book is a work of fiction. Names, characters, places, and incidents either are products of the author's imagination or are used fictitiously. Any resemblance to actual persons, living or dead, events, or locales is entirely coincidental.

Cover Design: Victorine Originals (ebook & print cover front) & Kristen Iten (print cover back)
Interior Design: Liwen Y. Ho
Publisher: 2 Square 2 Be Hip

First Edition

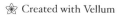 Created with Vellum

For my awesome Early Bird Launch Team members. Thank you for reading, reviewing, and believing in my stories. I am so grateful!

Chapter One

AIDEN

*a*iden Spark hunched over in his chair, his head in his hands. His cell phone dinged with another incoming text. *Ding, ding!* Two more messages came in, one after the other.

"Leave me alone," he muttered under his breath.

He picked up his phone and swiped open the text bubbles. As expected, he saw the names of his four younger brothers. They had even texted him in birth order.

Brandon: *Taking an editing break and thought I'd see how you're doing.*

Colin: *Stop by for ice-cream any day this week, on the house.*

Darren: *Praying for you in between calls today.*

Evan: *Sending you a hug from Hollywood, big bro.*

He imagined each brother texting him, then telling the next one down the line it was his turn. Actually, he didn't need to imagine it; he knew that's what happened. It had been the same drill every September fourth for the past decade. Ten years since the love of his life had passed away.

Swallowing past the lump in his throat, he managed to hold back his tears. It wouldn't do much for his professional life if his colleagues found him weeping during office hours. He already got enough slack for being the only male professor in his college's women's studies program. His female coworkers adored him. The male professors in the surrounding departments? Not so much.

His students, on the other hand, would probably fall over themselves to come to his rescue. He saw the way the female undergrads—who made up ninety-five percent of his classes—looked at him. His lectures were known for their near-perfect attendance, and he was sure it wasn't because the material was that fascinating.

The way he presented the material though? That's what drew people in. Being on stage was the only time he felt alive anymore. He taught with passion, but he also had what the tabloids once referred to as, "The Spark". A way about him that drew everyone's attention when he entered a room. Some called it charisma; others pointed to his smile and dimples. Whatever it was, made him the most popular teacher on campus.

At least one part of his life was going the way it was supposed to.

The other part of his life that hadn't gone as planned was memorialized in a single picture. He scrolled through his phone and opened the photo album. Mandy, his high school sweetheart, stared back at him, a bright smile lighting up her face. The photo was taken the day before graduation and the month before her diagnosis. Six months later, her beautiful brunette curls would fall out from chemo and the life in her blue eyes would disappear. A year later, she was gone.

Aiden rubbed one hand down his face, then wiped his damp palm along his slacks. He checked the time, noting his last appointment was late. It was better this way. Talking about women only reminded him of the one woman he had ever loved and ever would love. Maybe he was being melodramatic, but he couldn't change how he felt.

His brother Brandon joked that he should stop being a living, breathing Nicholas Sparks book, a love story with a sad ending.

It was a funny thing for a romance author to say. But Brandon wrote fictional stories with unrealistic, happily-ever-afters. Life wasn't like that. No, life gave you so many wonderful, unbelievable things, then snatched them away when you least expected it.

Aiden shook his head. *Stop it, that wasn't true*, he told himself. That's not what the Bible said. Even in Job's darkest times, he still believed God to be faithful and good. In his own life, he tried to believe it as well. Tried, being the key word.

He'd grown up in a Christian family with dedicated parents who not only taught him about Jesus, but lived out His teachings. He'd grown up in a loving, secure bubble, so much so that he struggled to stay upright once it burst. He'd had to rebuild his faith from the ground up after Mandy died, which had included a period of denying God. He'd partied too much and run with the wrong crowd, then left all of that once he hit rock bottom. Now, at age thirty-two, he was finally feeling more grounded. Except for that one day a year—today.

His phone rang with an incoming call. *Candace*. The name alone made him cringe. She'd already left him two voicemails. He answered, knowing he couldn't avoid her forever. She was as stubborn as her sister had been. "Hey."

A bubbly voice came over the line. "Aiden, hi! You finally picked up. Do you know how many times I've called you today? Two times before breakfast, once before lunch, and twice after. How are you, brother?"

As a food critic in the San Francisco Bay Area, Candace always talked in reference to meals of the day. She also insisted on calling him her honorary brother, even though he and Mandy never got the chance to marry. It was a kind, yet cruel, gesture.

"I'm great." He attempted to smile to sound happier than he really was. "How are you? What restaurants are you checking out today?"

"There's a French place that opened up not too long ago. It's in downtown Palo Alto, a couple of exits away from your school. You should check it out sometime. Bring a date."

He sneered at her not-so-subtle hint. Five years ago, she'd started pushing him to meet women, saying how it wasn't healthy for him to still be mourning her sister. Mandy would've wanted him to live his life, she'd reminded him. He resented the fact that she was right. Mandy had said so herself in their last conversation before she fell into a coma. Even still, he didn't care to move on.

"Thanks for the tip, Candace. Hey, sorry to cut this short, but I need to go. I have a student coming in for office hours."

"If you do, she's late," Candace retorted. "It's twenty-five past the hour and you only schedule appointments on the hour and never past three. If you want me to shut up and mind my own business, Aiden, just say so. I can take it. But before you do, let me remind you that Mandy wanted you to find love again. Don't forget you promised her you would."

"I ..." He rolled his eyes and sighed. She had to bring that up again. How much did deathbed promises mean, anyway, especially a decade later? Why wouldn't Candace accept the fact that he was fine being single?

"You're loyal to a fault," Candace continued, not bothering to let him finish his sentence. "That's something my sister loved about you. But Aiden, life is about going with the flow. Things happen and you need to make the most of the situation. And may I remind you again that you promised Mandy you'd move ... on!" She emphasized her last two words with a dramatic pause in between them.

"Are you finished?" Aiden dared to ask. Even though he'd studied women, it didn't mean he was an expert on them. Far from it. Growing up in a family of boys had taught him one thing: Never argue with a woman—ever. He believed in self-preservation.

"Yes!" Candace announced in a giddy tone. She paused and lowered her voice. "Look Aiden, I miss Mandy, too, every single

4

day. But there's a reason God still has us here. We have a life to live. Mandy lived hers to the fullest as she was able. You need to as well."

"I know." Of course, he knew it in his head. And a little bit in his heart. Eating dinner by himself every night confirmed why God had created Eve; it wasn't good for man to be alone. He did long for someone to share his life with. Maybe it was time to move on ... or to at least consider it. "I hear what you're saying and I appreciate it. I-I'll think about it. Okay?"

"That's the spirit!" Her zeal had returned in full force. "I'm so glad we had this chat, Aiden. I expect to hear updates on your love life the next time I call."

"I wouldn't get your hopes up—"

"I've been praying for you, brother. You know what happens when you pray, don't you?"

Aiden wouldn't know. He had stopped talking to God on a regular basis when God stopped answering his prayers about Mandy. But he knew the words to say. It had been Mandy's catch-phrase. "Hearts change."

"Exactly." Candace sounded pleased. "I'll talk to you soon, Aiden. Bye!"

He ended the call and shook his head. God help the man who ended up with Candace. He appreciated strong women—his own mother was one—but he had no idea what to do with them.

He checked his watch again. Three-thirty. He'd waited long enough for the student to show up. He checked the class list on his laptop and located her contact information. Squinting, he typed her number into his phone, along with the following message:

This is Professor Spark. You missed your appointment with me today. Let's reschedule for another time this week. Please text me back when you receive this. Thank you.

He reread the words, then hit the send button, not realizing how much this message would soon change the course of his life.

Chapter Two

ABBY

bby Dearan sat down in her black swivel chair and kicked off her sneakers. She took a long chug of coffee from her travel cup before setting it down. She said a quick prayer, thanking God for creating caffeine, because that was the only thing keeping her eyes open at the moment. She was used to starting her days in the radio station at five every morning, but it did take her a while to get into what she called her "deejay groove". Besides the long hours, she loved her work and couldn't imagine doing anything else. Who wouldn't love listening to Top 40 songs and chatting with listeners all day long?

After an hour of online research—checking out the latest celebrity gossip and prepping some giveaways—she heard loud footsteps enter the studio. She groaned inwardly. Her cohost had arrived. What used to be *Mornings with Abby* was now *Mornings with Marcus and Abby*. Ratings had gone up since Marcus came on board a few months ago, but it didn't make the change any easier to swallow. Abby had worked hard to get a solo gig and had been doing well until the producers decided to add some variety—mainly, a man's perspective—to the show. They said it was for the sake of bringing balance and to draw more male listeners. Apparently, Abby had been alienating them with her man-bashing. Was it her fault they couldn't handle the truth?

"Mornin', sunshine!" Marcus declared as he sat down beside her. "Any new prospects on the dating front?"

Abby turned to find her redheaded, blue-eyed partner grinning at her. She smiled back, trying to find it in her heart to show him some grace. She'd recently become a believer, kind of like beliebers who were dedicated Justin Bieber fans, but she was now a follower of Jesus. Thanks to her best friend, Danica's, patience over the years, she'd finally accepted God's unconditional love and forgiveness. Living it out, however, was an entirely different matter. She'd need a lifetime to figure out how to keep her snarky attitude in check.

Despite the fact he'd encroached on her workspace, Marcus wasn't a bad guy. Even though they were both thirty-one, he was like the older brother she never had. He'd recently gotten engaged and was now on a quest to help her find a man. He'd convinced her to sign up for three dating apps, promising they'd work for her as well as they had for him. She had to admit that while he was a good DJ, he was a lousy dating coach.

"Hey yourself. And no, there's nothing new to report, unless you're counting the fourteen winks I got, which hardly qualify as proper dating etiquette. What man goes around winking at women in real life? That would be totally creepy."

Marcus laughed. He squeezed one eye shut and asked, "You don't find this appealing?"

"It's a good thing our listeners can't see you." Abby rolled her eyes. "What happened to starting up normal conversations? One person says hi and the other person says hi back. A wink doesn't say anything, except for, I'm too chicken to talk to you."

"It's supposed to say, I think you're cute, and will you have pity on me and wink back so I know you're interested before I work up the nerve to send you a real message." He paused. "It might be hard for you to believe, but guys don't take rejection well."

She was about to roll her eyes again when something in her gut—or was it her spirit—stopped her. Okay, fine, men did have hearts, too. It was just that the men in her life had never cared about hers. Her dad had ditched her mom for another woman. One of her exes—the actor with a small role in a hit movie— dumped her during his fifteen minutes of fame because she wasn't pretty enough for the red carpet. If good guys still existed, she hadn't met one yet. Who knew if she ever would.

"Yeah, well, if a guy can't handle rejection, he shouldn't put himself out there in the first place."

Marcus winced. "Ouch. You don't mince words, do you? I sure hope there's someone confident enough for you out there in the world."

"I doubt it, but it doesn't matter. I prefer being on my own." She'd rather rely on herself—and God, of course—instead of another person. "Enough talk about my non-existent love life. Let's go over today's show."

"All right. What do we have on the agenda?"

Abby pointed to the websites open on the computer screen in front of her and began catching him up on the news. After another half hour of going over their talking points, they put on their headsets and turned on their mics.

"A happy Tuesday to you all in the Bay Area," Abby announced on the air. "We've got you covered for your morning commute. Don't touch that dial. Marcus and I have the latest headlines coming up at ten past the hour."

Halfway through their four-hour show, Abby got up to stretch. She took her phone out of her jacket pocket to check her texts. Her younger sister was starting a new job today and had promised to tell her all about it. There were no new messages, but there was an old one she'd received yesterday afternoon. She swiped it open and read it again.

This is Professor Spark. You missed your appointment with me today. Let's reschedule for another time this week. Please text me back when you receive this. Thank you.

It was obviously a wrong number. She should've deleted the text, but for some reason, she hadn't. Instead, she toyed with the idea of texting back. The professor sounded polite enough. The polite thing for her to do was let him know he'd reached the wrong person.

Abby twisted around to find Marcus peering over her shoulder. "Are you being nosy?"

"I was wondering what it was that had you so entranced. Did you get winked at again?"

"I'm hardly entranced. Curious, is all." She held up the phone for him to read. "I was debating whether to reply."

"A professor? I say go for it. The guy sounds nice. He's got good spelling and grammar, at least."

She wrinkled her nose. "What makes you think it's a man? A woman could very well be a professor."

He held up his hands in a sign of surrender. "Hey, I didn't say it was definitely a man. I just assumed—but you're right, it could be a woman. Either way, I'm sure he or she would appreciate a text back."

"Sorry, I didn't mean to bite your head off." Abby sighed. Why wasn't she gentle and peaceable like her sister? Not only had Emma inherited their mom's gorgeous red locks, she'd gotten her sweet spirit as well. All Abby had gotten was their good-for-nothing father's unruly dark hair, poor eyesight, and bad temper. She pushed up her glasses with the palm of her hand. "You're right, I'll reply." She paused. "You don't think this is a spam text, do you?"

Marcus shrugged. "Why don't you look the number up online?"

Abby returned to her seat, her curiosity growing even greater. "Good idea." She opened a new browser on her computer and punched in the professor's number. After a couple of seconds, a search result popped up. Pacific College in Palo Alto. That was only an hour away from their studio here in San Francisco, give or take thirty minutes, depending on traffic.

"It's a legit number," Marcus remarked. "If you want to be even more sure, go to the school's website and see if there really is a Professor Spark."

She was one step ahead of Marcus. She had already Googled the name, along with the college's name. Up popped a link to a page of faculty headshots, names, and job titles. The photo for Professor Spark was missing, but underneath the blank space, it read *Spark, Z., Assistant Professor.* "Whoever this person is really wants to remain anonymous. Everyone else has their photo and whole name listed. Don't you think that's weird?"

"Maybe they like their privacy. Plenty of stars are like that."

"That's because they have paparazzi following them twenty-four seven. Why would a college professor care?" Noting that the song playing on the air was almost over, she put her headset back on. "I bet there's a story behind this. And I'm going to find out what it is."

"Oh boy, I had a feeling you'd say that. So, you're gonna text him back?"

"Yup. Right now." Her thumbs flew over her phone screen as she typed out a sentence and hit the send button. When she finished, she held it up for Marcus to see.

His brows shot up as he read, "What class is this for again?" Shaking his head in disbelief, he remarked, "Ouch, that's kind of insulting. Now he thinks this student doesn't even remember who he is."

"That's the point, Marcus. How else will I get any answers?" She drummed her fingers impatiently on her desk. "Now I just have to wait for him to reply."

Marcus rubbed his chin. "There might be another way. I bet

you some of our listeners go to Pacific College. They could find out for you who this Professor Spark is."

Abby's eyes grew wide with delight. "Why didn't I think of that? Brilliant thinking, Marcus."

He winked. "Not bad for a guy, right?"

Grinning, she rolled her eyes. "Yes, but please stop with the winking." She then turned on her mic and announced, "Hey, 103.1 listeners, I've got a favor to ask you all."

Chapter Three

AIDEN

*A*iden eyed the cafe menu written in chalk on the far wall. He glanced at his watch, then at the front door. His brother, Brandon, walked in, right on time, which for him was usually ten minutes late.

Brandon greeted him with a wave as he approached the table. He gave him a quick hug and smiled apologetically. "Hey, bro. My treat since I'm late again. You want your usual?"

"Sure, thanks."

"All righty. One bacon, egg, and cheese breakfast sandwich and one medium latte coming right up."

"Thanks." Aiden watched his brother as he walked up to the counter to place their order. Only eleven months apart, he and Brandon had always been close, but his Irish twin was about as different from him as humanly possible. He was the only Spark brother to inherit their mom's blond hair and blue eyes. He was also tone deaf and time-challenged, as he liked to refer to his tardiness. But he was the brother Aiden felt the most comfortable with, which is why he'd dragged himself out of bed to meet up with him today.

Brandon soon returned with their food and placed it on the table. "Do you want to say grace, or should I?"

"You can do the honors."

Placing a hand on Aiden's shoulder, Brandon prayed, "Heavenly Father, thank you for this glorious day and for providing this nourishment for our bodies. I pray you would grant the same for our souls and help us know we're not alone. Thank you. In Jesus' name, amen."

Aiden opened his eyes. He took a bite of his sandwich to hide the smirk on his face. He appreciated Brandon's heartfelt words, but he'd heard them before and had yet to see them come to fruition. His soul felt as bland and flavorless as the eggs in his mouth tasted. The couple of days after the anniversary of Mandy's death were always a struggle to get through, and today was no exception. It usually took him a good week to get out of his funk. He swallowed and washed the food down with a long sip of coffee.

"So, how are you doing?"

He met his brother's eyes and shrugged. "Okay."

"Do anything ... different yesterday?"

"Not really."

Brandon opened his mouth as if he wanted to say something, then shoved his bagel into his mouth. After a few bites, he cleared his throat. "Can you believe it's been ten years?"

Aiden knew his brother had been working up the nerve to bring Mandy up. No one seemed to know how to talk about her anymore, if they should avoid the topic or dive head in. He preferred the latter. "Yeah. I got your text yesterday and everyone else's, too. Thanks for that."

"Of course."

"Candy called me, too." He shook his head in amusement, remembering their conversation. "I think she has too much time on her hands."

Brandon's eyes lit up at the mention of her name. "She makes time for the important things. So, any thoughts about what she talked to you about?"

His brother's casual tone didn't fool him. "No wonder she backed off so easily. She asked you to follow-up with me, didn't she?"

"She may have mentioned something about you needing a little push. And maybe a date," he added, along with a fake cough. "So, how about it?"

Aiden didn't like the grin on his brother's face. "How about what?"

"How about a little help getting back into the dating game?" Brandon asked in between bites. "Before you say no, hear me out. I know a great girl, her name's Danica and she owns a bookstore in Mountain View. She helped me when I did a book signing last month. She loves to read, and so do you—"

Aiden cut him off with a wave of his hand. "I appreciate the thought, Bran, but I don't think I'd be very good company right now. Classes just started and I've got a full course load, plus office hours." He realized he still hadn't heard back from the student who missed her appointment yesterday, and made a mental note to text her again. "Now's not a good time to start a relationship—"

It was Brandon's turn to cut him off. He narrowed his eyes and spoke in a matter-of-fact tone. "I'm trying to help you out, bro. If you agree to go out with Danica, Candy will get off your back. If you don't—" he shrugged "—well, don't say I didn't try to help. It's your choice."

Aiden palmed a napkin off the table and crumpled it in his fist. He didn't know whether to laugh or groan. From the way Brandon talked, one would think he was referring to a muscled firefighter like their brother Darren, not a five-foot-two woman. "Do you really think that's a credible threat?"

"Did you hear about the Italian restaurant that opened up a few weeks ago in Fremont?"

"Huh?"

"Exactly. You couldn't have because it shut down after Candy gave them a bad review. The woman means business, Aiden."

He scoffed. "Save the drama for your stories. I'll be fine. I won't pick up her calls. Problem solved."

Brandon cocked his head to one side. His brows suddenly quirked as he looked in the direction of the cafe's front door. "I wouldn't speak so soon. The *problem's* walking in right now," he muttered out of the corner of his mouth.

"You told her where we were meeting?"

"She caught me at a bad time. I was in the middle of writing a break-up scene when she called and I wanted to get off the phone."

Aiden heard the *click clack* of high heels approach before he caught a whiff of a floral-scented perfume. He looked up to find a pretty brunette grinning at them. "Candy, what are you doing here?"

"I was in the neighborhood and thought I'd drop by to see my favorite brother." She gave Aiden a peck on the cheek before sitting down. "So, has Brandon convinced you yet or do you need more encouragement?"

"I was telling him how busy I am with school. I don't have time to go on a date."

Arms crossed against her chest, Candy pursed her red lips. "Aiden, do you have time to eat?"

"I ..."

"Yes or no?"

"Yes," he admitted reluctantly, knowing exactly where she was leading the conversation. "But I take a lot of my lunches in my office. And I do a lot of prep work during dinner. There's not much time for socializing ..." His voice trailed off in resignation under her knowing gaze.

"But you do have time to go out for breakfast." She gave him a cheeky smile. She turned to Brandon and asked, "Would your friend be free for a breakfast date with Aiden?"

Brandon clamped his lips together to muffle his laughter. When he finally calmed down, he gave Candy a quick nod. "I'm sure she would be. I'll text her right now and set it up."

"Fine," Aiden cut in when he realized he wasn't going to get out of the date. "But make it dinner. Breakfast is too early for socializing."

Within ten minutes, Aiden had a date lined up for Friday night. And a throbbing headache. With any luck, it would turn into a full-blown migraine in three days and he could stay home.

Brandon and Candy left the cafe, but they both promised to check in with him. Aiden was sure they'd be texting him reminders about Friday. Candy had already offered him some outfit suggestions, and elastic pants were not an option. He glanced down at his gray sweats and sighed. It seemed like a lifetime ago when he'd cared about his wardrobe.

With only afternoon classes on Tuesdays, he decided to take his time going into the office. He swiped open his phone, debating whether to send a second text to the student from yesterday. He really didn't like having to hand-hold his students, but since it was only the second week of school, he'd give them some grace. He reminded himself it was best to give people the benefit of the doubt because you never knew what they were going through in life.

To his pleasant surprise, a message popped up on the screen. His delight soon turned into disgust when he read the text. Why, the nerve! Instead of apologizing, this student had the gall to insult him. He shook his head in disdain. Well, if she couldn't make the effort to remember which classes she'd signed up for, he wasn't going to do her any favors of reminding her. Smirking, he quickly typed out his reply—*The important one!*—and sent it into cyberspace.

His attention soon shifted to the catchy pop song playing

overhead. He found himself humming along, tapping his foot to the upbeat rhythm. Music always had the power to lift his spirits.

The fingers of his left hand began moving on their own, taking on different positions as if he were playing chords on a guitar. It'd been so long since he'd picked an instrument up, but some habits —or passions, rather—were hard to break.

Once the song finished, the smooth, lively voice of a female deejay came over the speakers. *Good morning, Bay Area! Abby here, with my co-host, Marcus. Thank you to everyone who called in yesterday to help me with my texting dilemma.*

The male deejay chimed in, *We've got the best listeners. They're all rooting for you to solve this mystery. Who is this mystery professor from Pacific College?*

Aiden's ears perked up. What in the world?

Abby continued talking: *For those of you who missed out yesterday, here's the scoop. I got a text from a professor asking me to meet him or her for office hours. Of course, it was sent to me by mistake, but I couldn't help wondering who this person was. I did what anyone would do; I did a Google search. Now here's the weird part. This professor is the only one on staff without a profile picture or first name listed.*

Marcus chimed in: *We're all curious now what he or she looks like. So, if you're a student at this school, or better yet, if you're a student of one Professor Z. Spark, give us a call.*

Aiden's jaw dropped. It couldn't be ... Were they talking about him? Heat rose up his neck as his heart rate picked up speed. He hooked a finger inside the collar of his polo shirt, stretching it out to cool himself off. Had he really texted the wrong number? That would explain why his student hadn't gotten back to him. But it would also mean his cover was at risk of being blown wide open. It would be hard to maintain his privacy if these deejays discovered he was Aiden Spark, lead singer of one of America's hottest boy bands from years past.

It wasn't hard to hide this fact from his students who'd been toddlers when Heartland climbed to number one on the Top 40 charts. Likewise, most of his colleagues had been too old to care. But these deejays were experts on the music scene. He'd done enough radio interviews to know it'd only be a matter of time before they figured out his identity.

So much for putting the past behind him.

Aiden gathered his belongings and headed out of the cafe. Ducking his head, he quickly got into his car and put on his shades. He turned on the engine and switched the radio to 103.1. The female deejay's excited voice filled the interior of his car.

Marcus! I got another text from the professor!

All right. Let's see if we can get to the bottom of Abby's mystery. But first, let's get an update on today's weather.

Aiden groaned and let his head fall back onto the headrest. This was getting out of hand. Wasn't there some juicy celebrity gossip to focus on instead of him? He dug his phone out of his pocket and swiped to his text messages. It was time to end this nonsense, once and for all.

Chapter Four

ABBY

*A*bby glanced up to see one of the producers giving her a thumbs-up through the glass partition of the studio. The production panel lit up like lights on a Christmas tree with all the phone calls coming in. This professor dilemma was working like a charm, drawing in almost as many listeners as the time she'd gone on a ranting spree about her ex-boyfriend. She shuddered, vowing to never air her dirty laundry on the radio like that again. It'd been next to impossible for her to get a date afterwards. That's why she'd resorted to online dating, where she could remain as anonymous as possible, separate from her identity as a man-hating deejay.

Her phone suddenly vibrated. No, could it be? The professor had texted her again! A giddy feeling shot through her body, putting a smile on her face. She felt like a teenage girl hearing back from her crush, which was a ridiculous notion, considering she had no idea who this Z. Spark was. It might be a middle-aged woman, or worse, a married man, for all she knew. But at least she was one step closer to finding out.

She announced the update to their listeners, then sat back as they cut to a commercial break. Swiping her screen open, she

19

proceeded to read the reply. She immediately scoffed. "Someone sure thinks highly of himself."

"Huh? So, you know it's a guy?"

"Let's just call it a gut feeling." Turning her phone to face Marcus, she gave him a moment to read the one-liner.

Marcus winced. "I hate to say it, but he has a right to feel insulted."

Abby shot Marcus a look that quickly silenced him. "I'll bet you, he's one of those scary professors who never grades on a curve." She wrinkled her nose. "He'd rather flunk half the class than give you a pass."

He shrugged. "Maybe. Either way, for the student's sake, you should reply and let him know it's the wrong number. We wouldn't want someone to really flunk the class because of this mix-up."

"Fine, okay." She began typing out a message, then stopped when three little dots flashed on her screen. Her eyes widened in surprise. "Hey, Marcus, he's writing me another text."

The following words showed up: *Please stop talking about me on the radio. I don't appreciate the publicity. You should have let me know I had the wrong number.*

Abby let out an exasperated huff. "No. Freaking. Way."

"Uh-oh, I know what those words mean." Marcus winced. "What happened?"

"Whoever this person is has the nerve to tell me not to talk about him on the air." She threw her free hand into the air. "Last time I checked, it's a free country. I have the right to exercise my freedom of speech."

He eyed her with a raised brow. "You're not going to let this go, are you?"

"What do you think?"

"I have to admit the whole mystery of this has been kind of fun, but there might be a good reason why he wants to remain anonymous. We should respect his wishes."

"And disappoint our listeners?" She checked the producer's notes on the computer screen in front of them. "We've got two people on hold who say they're in this professor's class. We have to take the calls, Marcus. Aren't you dying to find out who this person is?"

"All right, one call." Marcus pointed at his headset to remind her they were going on the air soon. After a few seconds, he updated their listeners on the situation, then took the first call in the queue. "Hi there, you're on the air with Marcus and Abby. Who are we speaking to?"

A young woman squealed with excitement. "I'm Jackie, a sophomore at Pacific College. Am I really on the radio?"

Abby adjusted her mic and joined the conversation. "Yes, you are, Jackie! So, I hear you have some insights for us about this Z. Spark. What can you tell us? Inquiring minds want to know."

"I don't know what Professor Spark's first name is, but I can tell you that he's pretty cool for an old guy."

Marcus chuckled. "When you say old, how old are we talking about? Fifty, sixty? Older?"

Jackie paused. "I don't know. Maybe forty? He still has all his hair and it's not white or anything like that."

"Girlfriend, forty is the new twenty. I wouldn't go around calling the man old yet." Abby made eye contact with Marcus and rolled her eyes. "Believe me, someday you'll be nine years away from turning forty and hoping no one refers to you as old. Anyhow, tell us more. What does he look like?"

"He's tall, dark-haired, and has a great smile. Ooh, and dimples, too."

"You don't say?" Abby remarked in surprise. "He actually sounds kinda hot. So, what class does this hot professor teach?"

"Intro to Women's Studies."

Both Abby and Marcus piped up at the same time.

"Excuse me?"

"No. Freaking. Way."

"Yes way!" Jackie replied matter-of-factly. "It's one of the most popular classes. I was on the waiting list all last year. I was so happy when I finally got in."

"Good for you. Thanks so much for enlightening us on this mystery of Professor Spark." Abby's cell phone buzzed again. While Marcus thanked Jackie for calling in and started the next song, she opened her phone to several new texts.

I asked you not to talk about me anymore.

Please respect my wishes or I will be forced to take other measures.

Really? Did this guy think he could threaten her into obedience? He didn't know who he was dealing with.

One final message popped up: *For the record, I'm thirty-two, not forty. But thanks for calling me hot.*

Abby snorted. So, the professor was hot and funny. *And* knowledgeable about women? Where did she sign up for his class?

"What's so funny?" Marcus peeked over her shoulder. "Other measures? Do you think he's going to call the police?"

She shot him one of her *oh really?* glares. "Please. What would the police do with his complaint? What we're doing is nowhere near being a menace to society. Quite the opposite. We're entertaining people. Something this professor obviously knows nothing about."

"Didn't the caller did say his class was popular? He must know how to draw a crowd."

"It's only because he's a young guy, and a good-looking one at that. Who knows if he really knows how to teach. He sounds like one of those artists who relies on their looks instead of their voice to sell records."

"Well, whatever it is, it's working. *I* almost want to sign up for his class."

Abby sneered as Marcus chuckled at his own joke. "Yeah, well, I would too if that meant getting a look at him. Hold on, isn't there another one of his students on the line? Let's ask her to take a picture of him and send it to us."

"Are you serious?"

"Of course. We need proof this guy's as hot as he says."

"He didn't call himself hot; you did."

"Argh, I did, didn't I?"

"Yep, you did." He leaned back in his seat and gave her a pointed look. "I think we've done enough digging. Let the man teach in peace."

"But this is a good story, Marcus. The listeners are loving it. We can't stop now." Especially if it meant she'd be on the losing end of this battle. She took a deep breath. Okay, maybe she was taking this whole thing a bit far, but she really didn't like being told what to do. If only that niggling feeling in her heart would leave her alone. Ever since she became a Christian, her conscience had been working overtime. The whole "love your neighbor as yourself" passage kept coming to mind. But this was for her job. She wouldn't do anything to prevent her neighbor from doing his. "I'm going to talk to the caller after this song's over."

Marcus shook his head in resignation. "It's your prerogative."

Yes, it was. Abby pushed her glasses up and squared her shoulders like she was about to face an opponent in a boxing ring. Scratch the boxing; a staring contest was more her style. Regardless, she was ready to fight.

Chapter Five

AIDEN

*A*iden took his place at the podium and switched on his mic. A sea of young, smiling faces stared back at him. His gaze swept the lecture hall, noting how it was completely filled. What the—? Even if all his students were to show up, there should still be extra seats left. He rubbed his chin, wondering if the recent turn of events had something to do with this.

It'd been two days since he'd texted the deejay named Abby, asking her to stop talking about him on the air. He'd tuned into the station for the rest of that morning to ensure she didn't mention him again. When she hadn't, he assumed she had complied with his request. However, something didn't seem right. Why was there a sudden boost in attendance? Even though his class was popular, the students tended to slack off on Fridays.

Still puzzled, Aiden opened his laptop to start his presentation. He greeted the students with a forced smile. "Good morning, everyone. I'm surprised to see so many new faces today. Just curious, how many of you aren't registered for this class, but are here to check it out? A show of hands, please."

Over a dozen young woman raised their hands. A small group of them were sitting in the front row, bright-eyed and attentive.

He pointed to one and asked, "Do you mind telling me what brought you here today?"

She batted her lashes and grinned. "I heard about you on the radio and had to come check you—I mean, the class out."

Giggles filled the room as other students nodded and murmured in agreement.

Aiden didn't know whether to be amused or disturbed. No, he was definitely the latter. And bordering on angry, which was one emotion he hadn't felt in a long time. Come to think of it, he didn't feel much these days other than sadness and loneliness. In a way, this was a welcome change. But he'd rather make changes on his terms, not someone else's. "So, you heard about me on Tuesday?"

"Nope, I think it was Wednesday."

The girl next to her piped up, "I heard them talking about you yesterday."

He balled his hands into tight fists. "Yesterday?"

Another student added, "They mentioned you this morning, too."

"I see." He took a deep breath and tried to stay calm, even as the muscles in his jaw tightened. It took everything in him to not pull out his phone and text the deejay right then and there.

But first, he had a lecture to give. Except he couldn't remember a single point he was supposed to go over. To buy time, he undid the buttons at the cuffs of his dress shirt. As he rolled the long sleeves up to his elbows, he quickly glanced through his notes. When he finally looked up, there were a couple of hundred students waiting expectantly for him. "Let's get started, why don't we."

Aiden had gone through a handful of slides when a student held up her phone and aimed it in his direction. Several more did the same, not bothering to hide the fact that they were not paying attention to his lecture. Kids and their electronic devices. He frowned. When did he start sounding like an old man? Probably since he heard one of his students refer to him as one on the radio. If only they knew how cool he had been back in the day.

Actually, if he had his way, they never would. He'd not only been cool, but selfish, too.

He raised his hands to draw everyone's attention. "I don't mind you coming today to check out my *lecture*—" he stressed the last word "—but I do have a "no phones" policy. This means no texting or calling in the auditorium. If you need to respond to a message, please step outside to do so."

The woman he had questioned earlier raised her hand. "Can we take pictures?"

"Pictures?" He glanced over his shoulder at the screen behind him. "Of the presentation notes? That's fine."

"Not of the notes," she replied glibly, "of you."

"What? Why do you want to take a picture of me?"

"Abby from The Morning Show asked us to get proof of your hotness."

His jaw dropped. It took a good long minute before Aiden composed himself enough to talk. "Please delete any pictures you took of me. Your parents are paying good money for you to come here and learn, not to play the role of paparazzi. If you disagree, you can take it up with the dean."

Whispers flew around the hall, but Aiden pretended to hear none of them. He didn't care that they now thought he was a hot, *grumpy* professor. He'd had enough of this deejay's antics. And he was going to let her know.

As soon as the lecture ended, Aiden retreated to his office. He turned on the radio on his desk and heard Mornings with Marcus and Abby still in progress. Sure enough, the deejays were talking about him—again.

A rush of heat flowed up his neck and into his cheeks. He was sure his face was as flushed as it had been in those awful tabloid photos from years ago; at least this time alcohol wasn't the cause. He'd stopped drinking after he crashed his car and narrowly avoided hitting a mother and her young children on the sidewalk. He'd done some stupid things when he was younger—most of which had been driven by grief—but there was no good excuse for his reckless behavior. Those were the memories he wanted to keep hidden. What would his colleagues and his students think of him if they found out?

He had to stop this Abby person from digging further. And there was only one way to do that. Call her up and talk some sense into her.

Picking up his phone, he dialed the station's number. When he got a busy signal, he ended the call and tried again. On his third try, he heard the phone ring.

On the fifth ring, a woman picked up. "Hi, thank you for calling 103.1. Who am I speaking with?"

"I'd like to talk to Abby. I don't know her last name, but she's the deejay on the air right now. This is important. I need to speak with her. Please."

"If you're calling in for the prize pack, I'm sorry to say you're not caller ten. Please hang up and try again. Thanks for calling."

"I'm not—" Aiden clenched his jaw as the line went silent. This station's staff was certainly efficient. No matter, he'd try again. He hit the redial button and waited.

The same woman answered. "Hi, thanks for calling 103.1. Who am I speaking with?"

"Don't hang up on me."

"Of course not, sir. You're caller ten. Congratulations!"

"What? Are you serious?"

"Yes. It's your lucky day. I'll need to gather some information from you so you can claim your prize."

Aiden rolled his eyes. Lucky day? Hardly. "I don't care about the prize. I want to talk to Abby the deejay."

"We'll get to that soon, sir. Now, may I have your name and the city you're calling from?"

"It's Professor Spark from Palo Alto. Can I talk to Abby now?"

"Professor Spark?" The woman gasped and repeated, "*The* Professor Spark? As in the one from Pacific College?"

"Yes, it's me. And I de—" He swallowed the word *demand*, choosing to keep his temper in check. He was so close to speaking to the deejay, he didn't want to risk coming across as a disgruntled listener, and lose the opportunity. "I *desire* to speak with Abby. Please."

"Certainly. Stay on the line; you'll be up next."

Now he was getting somewhere. He took a deep breath and waited. He heard the ending of a pop song play over the line, followed immediately by the first notes of another song. A very familiar melody. He couldn't believe anyone still played Heartland songs. It was a blessing and a curse his band's music had withstood the test of time. A young man started to sing, causing him to cringe. He never liked the sound of his own voice, especially the teenage version of it. He pulled the phone away from his ear for a moment, and nearly missed hearing a woman call out his name.

"Professor Spark? Are you there?"

He placed the phone back to his ear. "Yes, this is he."

The woman squealed in delight. "Professor Spark, am I happy to hear from you. You've been a hot topic around here."

"Yes, well, that's exactly why I called. I'd like to speak with Abby the deejay."

"You're speaking to her! But hold that thought." She paused before announcing, "We have a winner folks. It's our very own hot professor. Professor Spark, you are caller ten. Congratulations! You've won the prize pack ..."

Aiden glanced down at his desk, suddenly hearing Abby in surround sound. Her voice was coming from the radio and the phone. Was he on the air with her?

"Professor Spark, tell us, who are you going to take to the concert? Are you seeing anybody? Inquiring minds want to know."

"I, uh ..." Sure enough, his own voice was coming over the radio. He quickly shut it off. "Can I get off the air? I need to speak to you in private."

"Professor Spark, you must know all our listeners have been dying to find out more about you. You sound like quite a catch. Please humor us and share something about yourself. Just one interesting fact."

Aiden's face flushed again. Fine. If she wanted to hear something about him, he'd tell her. "I find your line of work demoralizing. You spend all your time gossiping about celebrities. Have you ever considered these are real people going through real problems?"

"Oo-kay. Someone's obviously not a fan of the entertainment industry. Which is what radio is all about, Mr. Spark." Abby's tone was light, but there was an edge to it. "If you don't like our commentary, you don't have to listen. Last time I checked, there are other stations out there."

He squeezed his eyes shut and took a deep breath. Had he chewed out a deejay on the air? What was his problem? Fine, he knew what the issue was. He had about ten years of anger at the media bottled up inside him, and it had sprung a leak. A very big one. He gritted his teeth. So much for steering away from arguments with women. He wasn't going down now without a fight.

ABBY

*a*bby shot up in her chair and leaned forward. Talk about being kept on the edge of her seat; she was there in more ways than one. She couldn't believe her luck—or was it providence? The very person she'd been hunting for information about this past week had called into the station. And she was speaking —er, arguing—with him on the air at that very moment. Adrenaline pumped through her veins as she anticipated the professor's next answer.

"Look," he barked, "no decent human being would exploit someone's weaknesses for entertainment's sake. There are more important matters going on in the world for you to talk about. You've been given this great platform; you should use it for good."

"Why I never," Abby huffed. Of course she knew what great opportunities her job offered. "I am using it for good! I support the arts, something you obviously don't appreciate."

The professor scoffed. "You really shouldn't make snap judgments like that. I have a family member in show business, and I fully support him. But I don't endorse all the lies and rumors the media spreads about him."

"You have a family—wait a minute!" Abby gasped. She

suddenly realized why his last name had rung a bell when she first heard it. "You're not related to Evan Spark, are you?"

"He's my youngest brother."

Abby turned to Marcus and pretended to fan her hand in front of her face. She raised her brows in delight. Evan Spark was one of Hollywood's rising stars who had landed a role on one of TV's most popular teen dramas. And he was hot. The teen in her swooned whenever he appeared on screen. If this professor was related to Evan Spark, he had to be handsome, too. "You don't say. Well, if good looks run in the family, then we won't need any photo evidence of your hotness. He's your youngest brother? How many brothers do you have? And are any of them single and over thirty?"

"There are five, but only two of us are—hold on," he stammered, "that's beside the point. We were talking about you and the media and the part you play in perpetuating gossip and ruining people's reputations."

"Ruining people's reputations? They do it to themselves. We only report it. It's news, plain and simple."

"That kind of information shouldn't be sensationalized. You're wasting your breath talking about things that don't matter. It's wrong, plain wrong. You should be shedding light on issues that will do good in people's lives, like raising money for cancer research. That's the kind of stuff that matters. Not the stupid mistakes a celebrity made when he was drowning his grief in alcohol." The professor stopped his rant and took a shaky breath. "Excuse me. I need to go."

"Go? We're just getting started."

"Please leave me alone."

Abby dropped her jaw. She sat frozen, her heart beating fast. She'd been going over her rebuttal in her head, but now she was listening to dead silence on the air. What had happened?

Marcus recovered faster than she did and quickly segued into the next song. He took his headphones off and blew out a long breath. "Score: Abby, one; Professor, zero. It's a shame. He didn't even try very hard."

"No, he didn't." She should've been happy the professor had given up. Then why did it feel like she'd been punched in the gut? She removed her headphones and got up from her seat. "I'm going to the ladies' room."

Shuffling her feet along the worn brown carpet, she made her way down the hallway. The building housed another non-competing radio station, and everyone was busy at work behind closed doors. She'd almost reached the restroom when her phone buzzed. For a split second, she wondered if it was Professor Spark sending her a text. She swiped the screen open and saw a new message from her sister.

Abby! You'll never guess who I met on set! EVAN SPARK. He's even more gorgeous in person. I told him you're his biggest fan. Gotta run. I'll text you pics later!

Abby slumped against the wall and laughed bitterly. Talk about coincidences. The one TV show Emma had landed a role on as an extra had to be Evan Spark's show. The brother of the man she had chewed out on the air. Chewed out to the point where Professor Spark's voice had fallen flat and been laced with sadness.

She shivered and wrapped her arms around herself. Even with a thick sweatshirt on, she felt a chill run down her back. She didn't want to acknowledge the emotion weighing on her heart. But the guilt loomed like a dark shadow, confirming how badly she'd behaved. Drat! She hated how sensitive she had become since receiving Christ.

Things that hadn't bothered her before now affected her in a big way. Every time a sentimental commercial came on, she had to change the channel. She'd even unfollowed the news on her social media feeds because they made her tear up. She supposed that's why she liked hearing and talking about celebrities. Their stories were usually fluffy and silly, unlike real life.

The professor's remarks pricked her soul. She had no clue what it was, but something had happened to the guy to make him so hopeless. She knew the sadness in his voice, the kind that ached with loneliness and regret. That was exactly what she'd tried not to sound like after her ex had cheated on her. Her efforts, however, had pushed her completely in the opposite direction. She'd gotten angry and vengeful. It was safer to sound strong than vulnerable, especially when thousands of people were listening to her.

She sighed. Now she not only felt guilty, she was down, too. She'd obviously stirred up some bad memories for the guy and pushed him into a corner with an audience listening. Fighting didn't seem so fun or effective anymore. That's the one thing she didn't understand about Jesus. How He had restrained Himself from fighting back at all the people who mistreated Him. He was God, yet He chose to humble Himself and die on the cross. The thought caused a lump in her throat. She swiped at her eyes with her sleeve. She sure could use a lesson—or a hundred—on humility.

She swiped open the messages on her phone again. Dreading what she needed to do, she began typing out a few texts, beginning with one to her sister.

Hey Em. You might not want to mention me to Evan. I'll explain later. Can't wait to see the pics.

Next, she sent a message to her best friend, Danica, the one person she always counted on to support her. They'd been roommates in college, and despite their contrasting personalities, Danica had always accepted her. She was the calm, level-headed one who'd stayed home to study when Abby partied all night long. And the one who had given Abby a Bible for her birthday and taught her how to pray.

Can you pray for me? I need to do something hard right now, but I know it's the right thing to do. Thanks.

Her phone immediately vibrated with an incoming call. Relief washed over her as she answered it. "Hey Dannie."

"What's going on, Abby? Are you okay?"

"You didn't happen to listen to my show earlier, did you?"

"Nope, sorry, not today. We're trying out a classical station. We had a customer complain that pop music was not conducive to reading. The point of a bookstore is to buy books, not read them in the store." She clucked her tongue in disapproval. "Anyway, did something happen on the show? Your ex didn't call in again, did he?"

"No, thank God." She rolled her eyes, remembering all the drama that had caused. "He didn't call, but someone else did. Remember the professor I told you about?"

"The one who texted you by accident?"

"Yeah. I might've made him cry on the air."

"What? You made a grown man cry?"

"I'm not certain he was crying, but he sounded really sad, which is making me feel really bad." Abby groaned. "You never told me becoming a Christian would make me so emotional!"

Danica chuckled. "It's a good thing. You're learning to have compassion toward others. Not that you weren't compassionate before, but now it's like a regular thing."

"Argh. The only thing I like having regularly is my coffee, thank you very much." Abby shook her head, then pushed her glasses back up when they slid down the ridge of her nose. "I think I need to apologize to him."

"The professor?"

"Yes," she squeezed out through gritted teeth. "I should probably text him back and apologize for being so pushy."

"Why don't you call him? Texting's so impersonal."

"What?! Calling's *too* personal."

"But it's more meaningful, right?"

Abby grunted.

"I didn't hear you," Danica teased.

"Yes, fine, I'll call him."

"You go, girl! I'll be praying for you." Her voice grew muffled for a second before she came back on the line. "After I ring up this customer. Gotta run. Love you, girl!"

"Thanks. Love you, too."

Abby lowered the phone and took a deep breath. She said a quick prayer herself and proceeded to dial Professor Spark's number. God help her, because she was going to need His divine intervention.

Chapter Seven

AIDEN

*A*iden smoothed the front of his light blue dress shirt as he glanced around the candlelit restaurant. Several well-dressed couples occupied the tables around him. Why had he let Brandon talk him into making reservations at one of the city's most romantic restaurants? Because, according to his romance author brother, he was supposed to make a good impression on his blind date. He released a long breath as he checked his watch. He'd rather be anywhere but here, especially after the morning he'd had.

His shoulders tensed just thinking about his conversation with that deejay. How had she ever gotten a job on the radio anyway? Other than the fact that she had a nice speaking voice, everything about her screamed *obnoxious*. He bet she picked a fight with everyone she met. People like her had to get the last word in. Well, not him. He'd chosen to back down rather than stoop to her level.

Fine. He hadn't acted that nobly. The truth was, he'd ended the conversation because he didn't want to fight. Thinking about the past—his mistakes and regrets—sucked the life out of him. He didn't want to get trapped in the vicious cycle of grief again.

He had work responsibilities to keep up with, bills to pay ... and this date to get over with. He owed it to Brandon after all he'd done for him. Plus, he needed to get Candy off his back.

He glanced around, wondering if his date had arrived. As he looked toward the front of the Italian restaurant, he saw a tall blonde woman walking to his table. Despite the nervous smile on her face, she gave him a quick wave. He rose to his feet and extended his hand as she neared. "Danica?"

She clasped his hand, staring at him with wide eyes. "Uh, yeah, that's me. Zachary, is it? It's nice to meet you. Brandon told me a lot about you ... but he may have left out some important details."

Aiden quirked his brow. Uh-oh. He had a feeling Danica may have been a Heartland fan back in the day. They were about the same age, after all. So much for asking Brandon to keep his identity a secret. He returned to his seat and tried to keep his expression neutral. "He told me some things about you, too. So, you own a bookstore?"

Her face brightened at his question. "Yes, I do. It's my pride and joy. I like offering people an alternative to online shopping. It's perfect for those who love to browse before they buy."

"That's great. Reading is a great form of entertainment."

She nodded. "The same way music is. Speaking of, we play a wide variety of music in the store. Sometimes I even put on oldie boy band songs from a decade ago," she added with a knowing smile.

"Oldie boy band songs?" Aiden didn't know whether to be offended or amused. He seemed to feel this way a lot lately. "I wouldn't call stuff from ten years ago old."

Danica laughed. "It is to the young people listening to it. I personally like the old stuff more. These days, it's more about an artist's crazy wardrobe or lifestyle than their music."

"I know what you mean." Aiden smiled. Maybe this date wouldn't be so bad after all. Danica seemed like a nice person, polite and courteous ... unlike some people he'd talked to recently.

He shook his head. Why was he thinking about the deejay again? She wasn't worth his time. Opening his menu, he directed his attention to the day's special. Strangely enough, his appetite, which had been poor all day, had returned. "So, what would you like to eat? I heard the shrimp scampi is good. A friend of mine's a food critic and she highly recommended it."

"That sounds great. I'll get that and a salad, too."

Aiden waved their server over and placed their order. Soon after, their salads arrived, and he gestured for Danica to start eating.

She hesitated for a second before asking, "Do you want to say grace for us?"

"I, uh ..." He swallowed hard. It was a simple request, but praying required faith, something he had little of since Mandy passed. He didn't want to fake a prayer though; he feared God too much to do that. He met her gaze and was surprised to see compassion, not judgment, in her eyes. "I'm not much of a praying person these days. Do you mind doing it?"

"Not at all," she agreed amicably. "Heavenly Father, thank you for arranging this opportunity for Zachary and me to meet. Please bless the food to our bodies and our conversation, too, that we would have an encouraging evening."

Aiden echoed her amen, mumbling it under his breath. He opened his eyes, suddenly feeling ashamed and out of his element. He was obviously not the right man for Danica ... or for any woman, for that matter. He wasn't in a good place spiritually. The man was supposed to be the leader of the family; his father had taught and demonstrated this to him and his brothers. At this point in his life, he admitted he wasn't ready for a relationship. He wasn't sure he ever would be. He picked up his fork and began eating, wishing the meal would be over soon.

They ate in silence for a while until Danica put her fork down. "You're not really what I expected."

"Huh?" He swallowed his mouthful of salad and asked, "What do you mean?"

"I expected pop stars to be full of themselves, but you're a regular guy. It's kind of refreshing."

"Oh. So, you do know who I am."

"Of course I do. I was a huge Heartland fan. I had your poster on my bedroom wall. You look the same, except for the facial hair and glasses."

He rubbed his goatee and offered her a grateful smile. "Thanks for following our music. As for the part about me being a regular guy, that's who I've tried to be since the band broke up. I'm not a pop star anymore, and I don't ever want to be one again. I'll be the first to admit I was pretty obnoxious when I was younger."

"Well, you're not obnoxious now. You're nothing like Brandon either, looks or personality-wise. That's probably why I never made the connection between you guys, even though you're both Sparks. Plus, he told me your name was Zachary. Is that like a stage name?"

"It's my middle name. It's what I go by now. Only my family calls me Aiden. I wanted to leave that part of my life behind me."

Danica's expression turned serious. "I understand. It seemed hard for you when the band broke up."

She had no idea. Even though the paparazzi had tailed him almost every waking moment, he'd managed to keep his relationship with Mandy out of the headlines. No one outside of his family knew her passing was the cause of his reckless behavior. "Yeah, it was rough."

They both grew silent until the server came by to deliver their main courses. Danica dug in to her pasta and exclaimed, "This is delicious! Your friend was right."

"Yeah, my girlfriend's sister has high standards when it comes to food."

Danica's eyes grew wide. "Your girlfriend? I thought Brandon said you were single."

"No, I meant my old girlfriend. I still keep in touch with her sister."

"Oh!" She smiled in relief. "Of course. That makes sense. I didn't think Brandon would set me up with someone already taken."

"Ah, no, he wouldn't. He writes romance, not drama. Although, I heard his latest book has some suspense in it."

"It does, and the storyline's so good." Danica's long earrings dangled as she nodded enthusiastically. "You know, I was so surprised when I met him for the first time. I always wonder if an author's like the characters he writes, so I thought he'd be this really deep and passionate person, but he's so down-to-earth, like the boy next door."

Aiden busted out in laughter, nearly spewing the food in his mouth. "Sorry, no offense to my brother, but he is the last person I'd call deep and passionate. I've never read his books, so I wouldn't know how he comes across in them. He has a good following though, so he must be doing something right."

"He's popular because most romance readers are women. You should've seen him at his book signing. He had all these lipstick stains on his face from the women kissing him! I had to use two face wipes to get them off."

"That's crazy. When Brandon was younger, he was so quiet and shy, he never even went to prom. He didn't have the courage to talk to a girl until his sophomore year in college. And that was only because she talked to him first."

Danica's eyes lit up in amusement. "That is so adorable. You can still see that part of him, especially when he's in front of a crowd. I practically had to beg him to read an excerpt from his book. He was so nervous, but he did great. He has such a nice, warm voice. I loved how he acted out the parts with so much conviction." She dropped her gaze as her cheeks flushed. "Anyway ... what were we talking about?"

Aiden bit back a grin. If he didn't know better, he'd say Danica liked his brother. Why in the world was she on a date with him then? "If you don't mind me asking, why did you agree to go out with me tonight?"

She winced. "Honestly? I wanted to help Brandon out. He's been pretty worried about you. He said it's been a while since you went out with anyone, and he thought I'd be a safe person for you to practice with. I hope you don't mind."

"I see." Funny how his introverted, play-it-safe brother was trying to help him out with his social life. "I guess I have been out of practice when it comes to dating."

"It's okay," Danica reassured him, "it's nothing to be embarrassed about. Life happens and we all get busy. Not to mention, it's hard to meet people these days."

"Yeah, I'm not really into the whole online dating scene."

"I get it. I tried a dating site once and it was like information overload. Who knows if half of what people say about themselves in their profiles is even true. I think meeting someone through mutual friends is the best way to go about it." She paused, then shot up in her chair with a big grin on her face. "You know what? I have a friend I'd love to set you up with. She was a big Heartland groupie back in the day and lives and breathes pop music. I'm sure you guys would get along." She grabbed her purse that was hanging on her seat back and took out her cell phone. "I can text her right now and ask if she's free this weekend."

Aiden held up his hand in protest. "I appreciate the thought, but I'm going to pass. I'm not ready to date right now. I-I think I need to get myself back on track first."

"Back on track?" She pursed her lips as she studied him. "Oh, you mean the praying thing?"

"Huh, you're quite perceptive."

She smiled. "It's one of my strengths. But back to you. I'm

glad you want to build up your relationship with God, but the thing is, sometimes it takes other people's influence on our lives to help us grow. We need others to push and challenge us. It's like what Proverbs says about iron sharpening iron."

A faint memory came to him of hearing a sermon once on that Bible verse. Something about people helping each other, much like the way rubbing two iron blades together made the blades more effective. While it sounded like an interesting concept, it also seemed like a lot of work. "Yeah, but I really don't have much time to date these days."

"But you do need to eat, right?"

He almost rolled his eyes. Did all women use the same lines? He gave her a curt nod, knowing his fate was already sealed.

"Great!" Danica beamed. "I'll set up a dinner date for you. I promise you'll have a good time with Gail."

Aiden wondered if there was some kind of conspiracy going on against him. By the end of the evening, he had a date scheduled for Sunday, his second one in a week's time. He sure was getting a lot of practice at dating, whether he wanted it or not.

Chapter Eight

ABBY

*D*rat! Abby cried out in pain as she accidentally skimmed the barrel of her curling iron against her hand. She dropped her arms and groaned. The reflection in her bathroom mirror was a hot mess despite her efforts for the past thirty minutes. She lifted her glasses with her palm and narrowed her eyes. Why did she bother anyway? She couldn't change what God had given her, even with the best beauty products.

She unplugged the curling iron and dropped it on the counter. Staring at herself, she ran through a mental checklist. Make-up done? If lip gloss and mascara counted, then yes. Hair curled? Kind of. Changed into something presentable? Most definitely yes. At least she'd gotten one out of three right. She smiled, admiring the blue dress she'd bought yesterday. The simple sleeve-less dress showed off her curves and didn't clash with her complexion. The silver cross necklace she wore completed the look, helping her look more prim and proper than she felt. Gentleness was not her forte, but maybe if she looked the part, she'd soon act the part as well.

Ever since she heard that morning's sermon from the book of James, she'd been convicted. Be quick to listen, slow to speak, and slow to become angry. Boy, oh boy, was that a message made for her. She'd be the first to admit that her mouth got her in trouble way too often. She had never cared about the consequences of her words, but lately, it was all she thought about.

Guilt certainly played a factor in her change of heart, but it was more than that. Living for Christ meant giving up her old ways and doing something better with her life. She wanted to be a blessing to others like Danica had been to her. If only kindness and compassion flowed out of her more naturally. Right now, it was a constant battle between choosing which shoulder angel to listen to. She still regretted that she'd listened to the bad one on Friday and hadn't gone through with apologizing to the professor. It wasn't her fault he hadn't picked up the phone, right? Um, yeah ...

Her cell phone rang, interrupting her visit to a river in Egypt, as she liked to call denial. She grabbed it off the counter and answered the call. "Hey Dannie."

"So Abs, are you ready for your date?"

"As ready as I'll ever be." She shifted her weight and leaned one hip against the counter. "Are you sure you can't tell me anything more about the guy? You can't say he's handsome and leave it at that. I want details, lots of them."

Danica chuckled. "I've told you everything I know. Well, almost everything. I don't want to say too much though; that'll take all the surprise out of it."

"It's already a surprise. That's what a blind date is, other than possibly the most humiliating social experience I'll ever have."

"You're being dramatic. Trust me. You're going to have a good time. He's a nice guy."

She scoffed. "That's what they say about criminals you hear about on the news. He seemed like such a nice guy. I never would've pegged him to be a—"

"Abby, stop! Please breathe. You have nothing to be worried about. Stop stressing yourself out."

"How do you know me so well?" Abby took a deep breath and exhaled, her cheeks puffing up like a hamster's stuffed with food. She crossed her eyes and shook her head at her own reflection. "It's been so long since I've gone out with a man. And I hate first dates. Hate, hate, hate! There's so much small talk about what you do for a living. Once they find out I'm a deejay, they start asking about all the celebrities I've met, and can I get them backstage passes to so and so's concert. You didn't tell him what I do, right?"

"Of course not. All I said was your name is Gail and you love pop music. He loves music, too," Danica added with glee. "You guys already have something in common to talk about other than work."

"Great, just great," she replied with as much enthusiasm as she could muster. Squeezing her eyes shut, she inhaled deeply, hoping the extra oxygen would calm her nerves. When nothing changed, she lifted her lashes and cried out, "What was that verse again, the one you told me about not being anxious about anything?"

"Philippians 4:6-7. Don't be anxious, be thankful, and present your requests to God. I'm paraphrasing, but that's the gist of it."

Abby nodded as she repeated the words to herself. "Easier said than done of course." She winced, her stomach suddenly cramping up. "I don't want to face rejection again."

Danica's voice grew soft. "I know. Believe me, that's the last thing I want for you, too. Which is why I chose this guy for you. He's mature for his age and he has a good heart."

"Okay, now he sounds like an old man, an old but healthy one. How do you know him again?"

"Through Brandon, the guy I met at the bookstore. Zachary's his brother."

"Ooh, Brandon the romance author. How's that going?"

"It's ... not. For someone who's so romantic on paper, he's kind of out of it in real life. I wish I were more outspoken like you. It'd make life so much easier if I could come out and tell him how I feel."

"Girl, consider it a blessing that you don't have a mouth like mine. You don't have to worry about offending people left and right."

"But it must be so freeing to be able to speak the truth."

"It's a blessing and a curse," Abby admitted. "I'm trying to work on the latter though. I'm determined to put today's sermon into practice. Starting with this date. I'm going to zip my mouth shut and for once, listen more than talk. Do you think I can do it?"

"Um, well, I think I know what *I* need to do tonight."

"What?"

"Pray for you," she answered matter-of-factly, before bursting out in a fit of giggles. "I'm so kidding!"

Abby rolled her eyes. "You're lucky I love you, Dan."

"I know. Love you, too, girl. I expect a full report later tonight." She paused. "I will be praying for you though. For both of you to have a good time."

"Thanks. Talk to you later."

Later that evening, Abby arrived at a steak and seafood restaurant in San Francisco. She carried her black clutch with one hand, while the other held onto the cross hanging around her neck. Taking a deep breath, she stepped inside, nearly stumbling in her three-inch heels. Her cheeks warmed from embarrassment. She almost turned to leave, but the attendant spotted her.

The middle-aged man in a black suit waved her over. "Good evening, miss. Are you meeting a young man here?"

"I-I think so. It's a blind date," she confided in a low voice. "His name is Zachary ..." She winced. With all the worrying she'd been doing over tonight, she'd missed asking Danica one important piece of information. "I don't know his last name."

"That's not a problem." He checked his appointment book and smiled. "Ah, you must be Gail."

"It's really Abby, but I go by Gail outside of work so people don't associate me with—" She shook her head in chagrin. Her nerves had her blabbing like a fool to a total stranger. She really needed to calm down and focus. What was that verse again? Oh yes, be slow to speak. She noticed the attendant waiting for her to finish speaking. She cleared her throat and nodded. "Yes, that's me."

"Right this way."

Abby followed him as he led her into the main dining room. She looked around the candlelit room and noticed several couples sharing intimate glances. The soft strains of a ballad played overhead and fresh flowers decorated each table. Everything about the place screamed—or whispered—romance. She loosened her grip on her necklace. This had to be a good sign, right? Only a decent guy looking for a commitment would pick a restaurant like this. Her eyes roamed the room, looking for a man sitting alone. She spotted one across the room.

The attendant turned back briefly and murmured, "The gentleman asked for a table in the corner. It's more private and offers a view of the bay."

She raised her brows. Wow, he was detailed and thoughtful, too? She nodded toward the man who had his head turned toward the window. "Is that him?"

"Yes. Are you ready?"

Good question. Was she ready? Abby chewed on her lower lip as she checked her date out. From what she could see, he appeared well-groomed. His dark brown hair was slightly wavy and cut short. He wore a light blue dress shirt paired with black pants that showed off a trim figure. And he was sitting up tall and straight. Wow. The guy even had great posture. So far, so good. She gave the attendant a quick nod. "As ready as I'll ever be."

"Good." The attendant winked at her. "I think you'll approve of his front view, too."

Abby let loose a nervous giggle. She quickened her last few steps to the table and waited as the attendant called for her date's attention.

"Sir, your date is here," he announced. "Your server will be by in a few minutes."

The man turned around and murmured his thanks as the attendant left. He rose to his feet to greet Abby.

As soon as Abby saw his face, her jaw dropped. No. Freaking. Way! Gone were the bleached blond highlights and round baby face, but she'd recognize those gorgeous green eyes anywhere. They belonged to the boy in the poster that she used to stare at every night before she fell asleep. Now they were fixed on her and causing heat to rise from her neck all the way up to the tips of her ears. She blinked quickly. What was the star of her favorite boy band, Heartland, doing here? Aiden Spark was her blind date?

Chapter Nine

AIDEN

When Aiden saw his date, his heart almost stopped. Mandy? He grasped the edge of the table, the linen tablecloth bunched up in his hands. He stared at her beautiful face for a moment before dropping his gaze. He shook his head. This woman had the same dark hair, oval face, and olive complexion, but she wasn't his old girlfriend. She came pretty darn close though. He'd always wondered what Mandy would look like if she were still alive, but he didn't need to wonder anymore. Whoever this woman was, she was the spitting image of her, wild hair and all.

He smirked, remembering how Mandy used to complain about how long it took to curl her hair. That was before she lost it and— He realized the woman was looking at him curiously. He quickly rose to his feet and extended his hand. "H-hello. I'm Zachary. You must be Gail? Please, sit."

She nodded and took the seat across from him at the round table. She fidgeted with her necklace before meeting his gaze. "It's so nice to meet you."

"You, too." Aiden was surprised at the tone of her voice. It was soft and sweet, almost breathless. Which was a good word to describe how he felt. He still couldn't get over how much Gail resembled Mandy. He found it hard to tear his eyes away, but he forced himself to. He handed her a menu and opened his own. "I hear the salmon is good here. I don't know if you like seafood or not."

Gail smiled enthusiastically as she perused her menu. "I do. I'll try the salmon."

"Great. Are you ready to order?" When she nodded in response, he called their server over. The young man filled their water glasses and took their order. When he left, Aiden directed his attention back to his date.

Seeing Gail did something to him. For the first time in a long time, he felt his spirits lift. He'd been so used to feeling sad, as if a dark rain cloud hung over his head all the time. Only recently did he start to feel something else—namely, annoyance. And it was all because of that deejay, someone he realized with dismay he was thinking about again. But today, right now, he felt excited, almost giddy. His heart seemed to thump stronger than usual, reassuring him he was still young and alive.

What an odd thought. He was nowhere near retirement, but he'd been feeling as weary as an old man. He should've been exactly the opposite—excited about life and looking forward to the future. Should, being the optimum word. A lot of things—his dreams, even his faith—had died a decade ago, along with Mandy. However, meeting Gail tonight not only gave him a sense of déjà vu, it brought him a renewed sense of purpose. Life wasn't over yet. For some reason unknown to him, God was still granting him breath. Maybe even a second chance at love? He pushed the thought aside. One step at a time. He needed to get to know this woman first.

"So, tell me about yourself. You're friends with Danica?"

"College roommates. Now best friends." Her eyes grew wide, and she grabbed her glass of water and took a long chug.

Was she nervous? He'd met so many female fans who'd had

trouble talking in his presence, he recognized the signs. The slight tremble in their voices, the inability to maintain eye contact, and the way their cheeks flushed when they snuck a glance his way. Check, check, and check. Gail had all the symptoms. Plus, an obsession with her necklace. She held onto the cross hanging from the chain like it was a lifeline. Perhaps it could be an icebreaker topic, a means to calm her nerves. He hated to see her so uncomfortable.

He pointed to her neckline and casually asked, "Are you religious? I noticed you're wearing a cross."

She opened her fist and nodded. In the next instant, she shook her head. "Not religious. I follow God, not rules."

"I see." He appreciated her straightforward response. She seemed to understand what faith was about; that made one of them. "That's an interesting answer. Don't you sometimes think though, it'd be easier to follow a list of rules?"

She took another gulp of water and pursed her lips. "Why do you say that?"

She was breathing like a normal person now. That was a good sign. Aiden decided to do his part and give her more than a pat answer. "Well, then we'd know exactly what we did wrong when we get punished. God says don't do A. You disobey and do A, then you get B, your punishment. So, if you don't want B, then don't do A. It makes everything nice and clear, don't you think?"

"I ..."

Before Gail could continue, he was already on to his next point. "But you see, if there are no rules to follow, you won't ever understand why you got B. Was there something I was supposed to do that I didn't do? Did God have a bad day and decide to take it out on me? You just don't know."

Gail opened her mouth, then shut it. She seemed to be holding back on saying what she really felt because she chewed on her lower lip until it turned white. After a moment, the line between her brows disappeared. "Tell me more."

"More?" Aiden blinked, not sure he heard her right. "You want to hear more about what I think?"

She nodded eagerly. "Yes. Please, go on."

He rubbed the back of his neck, chagrined. This woman was something else. Instead of telling him to be quiet or throwing a generic answer his way, she wanted to hear more. Not only did Gail resemble Mandy physically, she had the same heart as well. Supportive, patient, and kind. He swallowed hard. If he didn't watch out, he was going to fall for Gail—hard. "Um, thanks for the offer. It's been a while since someone cared enough to listen. My brothers try to, but you know how guys are."

"I wouldn't know. I only have a sister, and the guys I've known didn't stick around very long." She shrugged. "Enough about me. You were talking about your brothers?"

"Well, I've got four brothers and they're more comfortable offering solutions than a shoulder to cry on—not that I'm going to start crying on yours."

"I wouldn't mind. I'd be honored to have you cry on me." Her cheeks flushed, making her look like a shy, young girl. "That came out really weird. I don't usually go around offering my shoulder to men. I'm just excited to meet you."

Aiden nodded with a knowing smile. "Danica told you who I am, didn't she?"

"She didn't, but I recognized you when I saw you. You look the same as the last time you were on the Grammys."

"The same?" He chuckled. "You're being kind. It was over ten years ago. I'm pretty sure I've gotten older."

"Your voice has. It's a lot deeper and fuller."

"That's a nice way of saying I don't sound like a teenage girl anymore."

She grinned. "I liked how you were able to hit those high notes. No one else in Heartland sang like you."

"Because the rest of them went through puberty a lot earlier. My only saving grace was the fact that the fans seemed to like it.

It was hard for my band mates to make fun of me when there were girls screaming my name."

"I bet." She paused and narrowed her eyes. "It's none of my business, but why did you agree to a blind date? I imagine you could date anyone you want."

She sure thought highly of him. That, or she had some big misconceptions. "A lot's changed since I left the band. People haven't paid attention to me in a long time. As you can see, no one's lining up for my autograph anymore. Not that I want them to," he added quickly. "I'm done with that part of my life. I like my privacy."

"But what about the music, the performing?"

He shrugged. "I do miss it sometimes, but I'm out of practice. Honestly, I haven't picked up a guitar since that Grammys show."

"Are you serious? But you were amazing at it. The songs you wrote were the best. They get requested all the time at—on the radio. I still listen to Heartland's greatest hits album."

"You do?" Their eyes met across the table, and Aiden was surprised at the connection he felt. He'd never believed in love at first sight, but the spark between them was too strong to deny. Maybe the theory did apply in this case. After all, Gail resembled Mandy in so many ways, it was almost like he'd known her for half his life. And, he discovered with a contented sigh, he wouldn't mind getting to know her better. He liked who he was when he was with her. "Thanks, I appreciate it. Maybe I'll start playing again. Just for fun."

She smiled. "Good. I'm glad to hear that."

The server arrived to deliver their food, forcing them to break off their gaze.

Aiden enjoyed watching Gail's reaction as her plate was set before her. The way her eyes widened upon seeing the artistic plating of the salmon and vegetables delighted him. He responded in a similar fashion when his own meal of prime rib and potatoes was placed on the table. The smell of spices reached his nose, causing his stomach to growl. His appetite had been returning in the last few days, and today was no exception. The delicious meal, plus the company of a beautiful and sweet woman, was sure helping to bring him out of his funk. He felt so energized, he considered saying grace. After all, he was thankful for the meal. He didn't need to have everything figured out to tell the Lord that.

"I can pray for us."

"Sure, thank you."

He bowed his head and closed his eyes. The words came to him from rote memory as he murmured a quick word of thanks. When he looked up, Gail offered him an appreciative nod as she picked up her fork.

The two of them sat in silence as they ate. There was no awkwardness though; it was what Aiden remembered experiencing with Mandy, a comfortable calmness of being with an old friend. He stole a glance Gail's way as he cut into his steak. He didn't realize he'd been staring at her until she stopped eating.

"What's wrong?" She covered her mouth with one hand. "Do I have food on my face?"

"No, you're fine. I can't get over how much you remind me of someone I used to know."

"I hope it's in a good way," she murmured, her mouth now hidden behind her cloth napkin. Her brows drew together as she added, "And not because I'm a messy eater."

"You're not messy at all. In fact, you look beautiful."

Flustered, she lowered her gaze. "You don't have to say that."

"But I mean it." He lowered his voice as he confided in her. "I was feeling nervous about coming here tonight, but as soon as I saw you and we started talking, the nerves went away. I'm really happy to be on this date with you, Gail."

Her eyes lit up. She dropped her hands to reveal a look of relief and joy on her face. "Same here. I'm so happy, too," she gushed, before punctuating her statement with a wide grin.

That's when Aiden saw the remnants of green food—likely spinach—lodged between her two front teeth. He winced, knowing he needed to bring it to her attention. "Actually, you do have something in your teeth—"

Gail clamped her lips together and shot to her feet. "I'll be right back," she mumbled out of the corner of her mouth.

Aiden nodded as his date scrambled quickly to the ladies' room. Hopefully this would be one situation they'd laugh about later. The thought filled his heart with joy. It was nice to finally have something to look forward to again.

Chapter Ten

ABBY

*D*arn spinach! Abby stared at her open-mouthed reflection in the restroom mirror and almost cried. Of all days to have food stuck in her teeth, it had to be today. On her date with the most amazing man in the world. The teenager in her wanted to squeal for joy, while the grown-up in her furiously searched her purse for floss. Her hand bumped against a small white container, which she fished out with a cry of delight.

A woman stepped out of one of the stalls and gave her a curious look. "Are you okay?"

With several fingers in her mouth, Abby responded with an eager nod. She flossed her upper front teeth, then decided to do the rest of her mouth. She decided that if she needed to, she'd drink water for the rest of the meal to prevent any further moments of embarrassment.

Why had Danica not told her she'd be seeing the man of her dreams? Heartland had been her favorite boy band growing up, and the lead singer was everything she ever wanted in a boyfriend. Charming, considerate, and musical. Most importantly, he was a believer. He seemed like the perfect guy.

What was it about men? They aged so well, and Aiden was no

exception. She'd had a hard time breathing and thinking when he was only a foot away. She'd almost given up on speaking, too; it was so difficult connecting her words from her head to her mouth. That's why she'd let him do all the talking, which had been part of her plan to begin with anyway. If only Danica could see her. She'd be so impressed by how she'd kept her mouth shut. Oh, but she was ready to give a mouthful to her best friend for giving her the biggest shock of her life.

Abby threw away her used floss and washed her hands. She dug her phone out of her purse and swiped it open to call Danica. Her friend picked up on the second ring. "What in the world were you thinking when you set me up on this blind date?"

Danica responded with a chuckle. "Hey, Abs. I have two words for you. You're welcome!"

She rolled her eyes. "How could you not have prepared me for this? I was freaking out when I saw it was—" She turned her back on the woman who was now using the sink beside hers. The last thing she needed to do was let the whole world know she was on a date with a celebrity. Lowering her voice, she continued, "Aiden Spark. You know how much I love him!"

"Which is why I couldn't tell you ahead of time. I didn't want you to worry more than you already were." She paused. "Do you forgive me?"

"Forgive you? I love you, girl! This is the best night of my life. My inner teen is doing a happy dance right now." The tapping of her heels echoed in the restroom as she shimmied in place. She held back her emotions until the other customer walked out. As soon as she was alone, she let out a wild yelp.

"Abby! Are you okay? I take it the date's going well?"

"Oh my goodness. He's so gorgeous, but not only that, he's so sweet. And he called me beautiful. Can you believe it? Aiden Spark thinks I'm beautiful!"

"Wow, he sounds a lot more animated than he was on our date —I mean, the time we met."

"You went on a date with him? You didn't tell me that."

"It was totally platonic. You know I like Brandon, so when he asked me to do this favor for him, to help his brother get back into the dating field, I said yes. We did not hit it off though. To be honest, he was pretty withdrawn on our date. He hardly made eye contact. I thought he needed someone like you to draw him out of his shell. Looks like you did the job."

"Hm, I guess I did." Abby placed a hand on her hip as she pondered Danica's words. "But what you described doesn't sound like the same man I'm with tonight. Well, other than the fact that he was a little moody at first. He seems really eager to get away from his past. He doesn't care about his celebrity persona at all. He even introduced himself with a fake name." Abby almost dropped her phone. "Oh nooo ... You've got to be kidding me!"

"What's wrong? What are you talking about?"

Abby gasped and held onto the wall to keep from falling over. "Dannie, you're not going to believe this."

"What is it? Tell me!"

"Why, oh why?" Abby moaned. Of all the people she had to go yell at on live radio this week ...

"What's going on? Did he freak out or something when you told him you're a deejay?"

That was exactly the problem. All the pieces started falling into place in a strange, convoluted way. And she couldn't wrap her mind around how crazy it all was. "You remember the professor I told you about? The one I got into a fight with on the air?"

"Yes? What does he have to do with this?"

"His name was Z. Spark. Aiden introduced himself as Zachary. Both Aiden and Zachary come from a family of five brothers. And they both like their privacy. This is way too much of a coincidence." Abby sucked in a deep breath, her heart pounding in her chest. "I think Aiden Spark and the professor are one and the same."

"What? No—"

"Freaking. Way?" She threw her hand up in the air. "Of course this would happen to me. I meet the man of my dreams and it turns out he hates me."

"I wouldn't go that far. He doesn't hate you."

"Oh, yes, he does. He likes Gail, but he hates Abby." She shook her head so hard, her glasses shifted on her face. "What am I going to do?"

"Well, you should probably confirm his identity first. What if he's not Professor Spark?"

"And what if he is? I'm ninety-nine percent sure he is." She released a heavy sigh. "Can I not tell him who I am?"

"Um, he's going to find out sooner or later."

"I know, I was only kidding. Argh. This whole date is ruined now. Why couldn't I have one nice evening out?"

"The night's not over yet, Abby. You could still have a great time."

"Like that's going to happen. Not after he finds out I'm the deejay who dissed him." Abby slumped against the wall, her knees buckled together. "I feel so bad. Now I completely understand why he was so upset that day about the media and why he hates celebrity gossip. I would, too, if I were him. I shouldn't have been so hot-tempered. I should've kept my big mouth shut."

"It's okay. You can't change what happened, but you can make up for it. Hey, look at it this way. This is God's way of giving you a chance to make amends. I'm sure Zachary or Aiden—whatever name he goes by—will understand."

"I don't know." Abby straightened and took a deep breath. "Please keep praying for me, Dannie. I really, really need all the help I can get."

"Of course. Remember the verse we talked about earlier? Don't worry about anything, but in everything—you know what, let me text it to you. As soon as we hang up, I'll send it over."

"Thanks, I appreciate it."

Sure enough, thirty seconds later a new message popped up on her phone screen. Abby read it over and over, committing the words to memory. She said a prayer herself, presenting her requests to God and thanking Him as well. As she was about to thank Danica, another text came in.

She swiped it open and saw a photo of a pretty red-haired woman's smiling face next to a handsome young man's. Talk about six—or in her case, two—degrees of separation. What were the chances both she and her sister had met a Spark brother in the same week? Boy, did she have a story to tell Emma later. Fingers crossed, it would be one with a happy ending, one they would all laugh about one day. Anything was possible for God, right? He'd created the whole universe from scratch, after all. He could help Aiden forgive her, right?

Swiping one text thread closed, she opened another to reply to Danica. *Here I go. Please pray Aiden or Zachary doesn't hate me after I tell him who I am. Thanks.*

Abby tucked her phone back into her purse and smoothed the front of her dress. After taking one last look at herself in the mirror, she stepped out of the restroom. She dragged her feet as she walked as slowly as possible back into the dining area, her eyes trained on the plush carpet beneath her heels. As she neared the corner of the room, she glanced up, then gasped. The seat where Aiden had been sitting was now empty, and he was nowhere to be seen.

Chapter Eleven

AIDEN

*A*iden rolled over in his bed, willing sleep to come. In his rush last night, he'd forgotten to close his curtains. Sunlight now streamed in through the window, ushering in the day far too early. Outside, a neighbor's dog was barking, taking on the roles of honorary guard dog and alarm clock. His townhome complex in the heart of Silicon Valley had been advertised as quaint and welcoming, but this morning it was anything but. He threw off his covers and groaned. What a way to start the week. He had a long Monday ahead of him and no energy or motivation to get through it.

He sat up, his eyes sweeping over the master bedroom. He had to admit that even though he wasn't a celebrity anymore, he still lived like one. When he bought the unit five years ago, he'd splurged on plush carpeting and matching, high-end furniture. His closet was full of brand name clothing, all of which were regularly cleaned and pressed by a laundry service. He even employed his own housekeeper who shopped for him and took care of the home.

The only service he no longer used was a driver and that was because he'd bought his dream car, an Aston Martin, and wanted to drive himself around. He also had enough electronic gadgets to fill up his bachelor pad, everything from drones to multiple video game consoles to a state-of-the-art sound system. That's what a single guy did with the royalties from four hit songs he'd written. There was pretty much nothing he kept himself from buying, partly because he could and partly because he had nothing else to spend his money on. If he had a wife though, it'd be a different matter.

His gaze landed on an 8x10 framed photo displayed on his nightstand. The picture was taken on the same day as the one of Mandy that was stored in his phone. He had his arms wrapped around her in a tight embrace as the two of them stared into each other's eyes. Everything about the day had been perfect, from the warm weather to their conversation after the photo shoot.

Even though they were only eighteen, they'd talked about marriage. He'd had it all planned. Mandy would go to college and become a teacher; he would continue writing songs and performing with the band. They'd spend the summers together. After a couple of years, she'd graduate, they'd marry, and she would go on tour with him. In their young, idealistic minds, they had been determined to live out of suitcases, because who cared about luxury if they had each other? That had been the plan. Now he had all the material things, but no one to share his life with.

Why had God's wrath fallen on him? Why did Mandy have to die and his plans get derailed? Had he been too self-centered when he was younger? Maybe he had flirted with too many fans. But what teenage boy, especially a pop star, wouldn't crave the attention of millions of girls? If only he understood what he'd done wrong. The guilt he felt over Mandy's death still ate away at him all these years later. He'd never told anyone how he felt, and he couldn't believe he'd finally verbalized his doubts last night. But of all the people to open up to, it had to be *her*.

The woman he'd been so thankful to meet yesterday had turned out to be the one woman he couldn't stand. Funny how everything had changed in a matter of minutes. All because of a single text message.

Aiden reached for his cell phone sitting beside the photo. One swipe of his screen revealed the source of his restless night. He still couldn't believe it. Gail was the deejay. What kind of game was she playing? Had she told Danica to arrange the date as some secret ploy to get an interview with him?

Even worse, why was God messing with his heart? Getting his hopes up by bringing Gail—or rather, Abby—into his life, only to crush them to the ground? He ran his hands through his hair, pulling at the ends in frustration. So many questions and no plausible answers. Nothing made more sense today than it had yesterday. In fact, he felt more conflicted than ever.

He replayed the memory of the moment he'd gotten Abby's message. He'd been confused at first why the deejay was texting him again, then it took but a few seconds for the pieces to fall into place. That's when he'd gotten up as quickly as possible, but not before he spotted Abby walking back to their table, head down with one hand clutching her necklace. He ducked out of the restaurant soon after, but the image of her slumped shoulders stuck with him, piercing his conscience. Why exactly, he didn't know. Or rather, he didn't want to admit the reason. He hated the fact he had stood her up, that he'd been a coward. What kind of man left his date without warning and to foot the bill, no less?

He was a coward *and* a jerk.

What was he supposed to do now? Move on and forget the date ever happened? Demand an explanation? It all seemed useless. He was done with this nonsense and done with this deejay.

But it seemed she wasn't done with him. He noticed three flashing dots pop up in the message thread. Was Abby texting him again? What could she possibly have to say to him? He soon found out when a new text came in.

Aiden, while I didn't appreciate you leaving me at the restaurant last night, I understand why you did.

I promise you I had no idea who you were before we met. It was not some secret ploy to meet you or interview you. I may be a fan, but I'm not crazy or desperate.

It was a weird coincidence or maybe divine intervention. Anyway, I wanted to apologize about the things I said on the air. It wasn't nice or fair of me.

I'm sorry.

The messages ended, but Aiden kept rereading them. Divine intervention? Yeah, right. He didn't know about that part, but the other things Abby said seemed true. She'd apologized, too. It was more than he'd be willing to do under the circumstances. He sighed. The least he could do was acknowledge her effort. He typed, *I accept your apology,* and hit send.

He threw the phone on his bed and went about his morning routine. He showered and changed into slacks and a dress shirt in preparation for his lecture later that day. Deciding to grab coffee and breakfast on his way to work, he gathered his belongings together, including his phone. That's when a new text from Abby appeared.

Okay, it's your turn now.

His turn? He sent back a simple two-word answer: *For what?*

To apologize!

Aiden dropped his laptop bag onto the carpet. Apologize? The nerve of this woman. Who did she think she was, demanding his apology?

His thumbs flew over the screen as he typed out a response. *Why do I need to apologize? You're the one who lied to me. You called yourself Gail. How was I to know you were the deejay?*

Those three dots appeared again, making his jaw tighten. So, she wanted to play, did she? He stared at the screen in antic-ipation.

You're one to talk! You called yourself Zachary! You're just as guilty of lying.

Aiden's neck heated under his collar. He undid the top few buttons of his shirt and sat down on his bed. He had a feeling Abby was only getting started. He was right. Another message immediately popped up.

And to think I was feeling bad for the way I treated you. At least I had the courtesy to admit when I was wrong. You think you're above everyone else because you're a celebrity.

I told you I'm not a celebrity anymore, he typed. *I just don't appre-ciate being lied to.*

I didn't lie! Gail's a name I use so people don't know I'm Abby the deejay! I hate it when people start asking me for favors when they find out I work for a radio station.

Aiden scoffed. *You do admit you were hiding your identity from me.*

A minute passed with no response. He wondered if Abby had given up. Before he could celebrate his victory, his phone rang with an incoming video call. The word *Deejay* flashed across the screen, identifying the caller. No way. What was she up to now? He swiped the phone to answer the call.

A familiar face showed up on his screen. Her cheeks were rosier than they were last night, but there was the woman who looked so much like his Mandy. But she was nothing like her. Even still, Aiden's chest constricted to see her face again. He brushed his fingers across the screen and swallowed hard.

Abby's expression softened for a moment as she stared at him from the screen. Concern flickered in her eyes when she spoke. "Aiden?"

Flipping the screen around, he wiped his eyes. When he turned the phone back towards himself, he set his jaw and gave a curt nod.

"Are you okay?"

The tenderness in her tone caught him off guard. He shook his head to clear his wayward thoughts. No matter how much Abby reminded him of Mandy, she wasn't the woman he once loved. He focused on the rounded corner of the phone to avoid meeting her gaze. "I don't have time for this. Let's call it even and be on our way. I don't want to see or hear from you again."

"What gives you the right to tell me when it's over? It's so not over. You left me with a huge bill. You could've offered to pay half of it. I wasn't the one who ordered a $48 ribeye."

"What happened to it?"

"The bill? I charged it to my credit card. I didn't have that much cash on me."

"Not the bill," he snapped, "the ribeye."

"I took it home of course. There was no way I was going to leave it sitting untouched on your plate. After everything the cow went through for your meal, the least I could do was enjoy it."

"That settles it then. You ate it; you pay for it. I don't see why I have to."

She snorted. "Are you kidding me? You picked the fanciest restaurant in town and ordered one of the most expensive dishes on the menu. You think because you can afford an extravagant meal, everyone else can, too?"

Aiden opened his mouth to answer, but soon realized it was a rhetorical question when she didn't pause a beat.

"Well, listen up, buddy. I'm not rich like you. I don't even like steak, especially when it's pink in the middle. I had to nuke that baby until it was well done. It made for a great midnight snack, but it was not worth $48 of my hard-earned money. But you obviously wouldn't understand any of this because you're a celebrity who couldn't care less about us little people!"

Did she not listen to anything he said? "I told you I'm not a celebrity!"

"Oh, please," she barked. "You are too a celebrity and the worst kind there is! You only care about yourself. I can't believe you dissed me for not caring about people! I doubt you use your fame or money for good—"

He'd had enough. He hit the button to end the call. Who was she to judge him?! He was done with the deejay. It was time to move on, even if he had nothing to move forward to. Living in the present was still better than being stuck in the past.

Chapter Twelve

ABBY

Oh, the nerve of that man! Not only did he ditch her at the restaurant with a gigantic bill, he'd hung up on her, too! And to think she'd been so enamored with Aiden Spark. He was the last person she wanted to be around. He was rude, conceited, and moody.

Abby drummed her fingers on her desk, the furious pace matching the annoyance building in her body. She thought she was temperamental, but Aiden took the cake. One minute he was ready to fight; the next minute he looked like he'd lost his best friend. Whatever was going on with the guy was too much for her to handle. Good riddance. That was the last time she dealt with a celebrity outside of work.

"Trouble in paradise?"

Abby turned around in her swivel chair to find Marcus grinning at her. "Don't even get me started." She planted her sneakers on the floor to push her chair around again, then stopped. Her blood was boiling too much now. If she didn't vent her frustrations, she'd be a ticking man-hating time bomb on the air later. It was the last thing she needed. She faced her colleague again and raised a brow. "Since you asked ..."

"Oh, boy, I know that look." Marcus shifted in his seat. "Let me get comfortable. I have a feeling this may take a while."

"You have no idea," Abby began. She filled him in on every-thing that had happened the previous evening and that morning. The more details she gave, the farther Marcus's jaw dropped, until his mouth was a gaping round hole. When she finished her spiel, she crossed her arms and groaned. "Why me, Marcus? Why?"

"I still can't get over the fact that you went on a date with Aiden Spark from Heartland. He was one good-looking kid. What does he look like now?"

"Focus, Marcus! It doesn't matter if he's more gorgeous than ever—" she pushed the image of his breathtaking smile out of her mind "—because he's a jerk. I can't believe I thought we had a connection. I was completely blinded by his voice, his dimples, and that adorable goatee of his. Argh! I don't even like facial hair on a man."

Marcus laughed, then clamped his mouth shut when she glared his way. "I don't think a voice can blind you, just saying. A voice can make you deaf, but it can't affect your vision—okay, you get my point. So, you were attracted to him; that's no surprise. I know how much you love the band and their music. But when you say connection, was it physical or something more?"

"I-I don't know and I don't care," she decided. So what if she'd felt strangely at ease with Aiden Spark. What did it matter that he'd looked at her with such tenderness in his eyes and called her beauti—no, stop! Abby pinched the bridge of her nose under her glasses. "I'm going to forget all this ever happened and move on. Thank God I won't ever have to see or talk to that man again."

Or so she thought, before she received a call from her sister that afternoon on her drive home.

"Hey, Em, how are you? Sorry I haven't texted or called you back; it's been crazy." A high-pitched squeal came over the line, making Abby pull the phone away from her ear. "Uh, Emma?"

"He asked me out, Abby! Evan Spark asked me out!"

No. Freaking. Way. Why wouldn't the Spark family leave them alone? "Emma, you listen to me. If Evan Spark is anything like his brother, Aiden, you need to stay away from him. Aiden Spark is nothing but a rude, obnoxious jerk."

"Aiden Spark? As in the guy you used to have a poster of on your wall? Evan didn't tell me his brother was in a boy band."

"See, he's lying to you already. Don't say I didn't warn you. These Spark brothers are trouble. As your big sister, I'm warning you to stay away from him."

Emma laughed. "I wouldn't call it lying. We only met a few days ago. I'm sure there's a ton of stuff he hasn't told me yet. But what's going on with you and his brother? When did you meet him and how?"

Abby gritted her teeth. She slammed on the brakes and narrowly missed hitting a black SUV limo in front of her. The streets in San Francisco were jam-packed already at five in the afternoon with people trying to get out of the city. In her old clunker, she felt like a little fish swimming in an ocean of bigger fish, trying to make her way through the current. It wasn't fair other people, like those in the vehicle in front of her, had it so much easier. They had their own pool to wade in, a special one with chauffeurs. That was a pop singer's life, not hers.

No wonder she and Aiden didn't get along. All that going back and forth about who should pay for a pricey cut of beef proved it. He was used to the royal treatment and having everyone think he was the best thing since sliced bread. Well, no more. He'd lost her as a fan, once and for all.

She didn't find him even mildly attractive anymore. She knew the real person behind the pop star persona, and she was sorely disappointed, even disgusted. The real Aiden Spark was a sad, sad man who didn't deserve a second more of her time. She didn't even want to waste her breath talking about him. "It's a long story and I'd rather not go into the details. He already ruined my whole morning and now I'm spending a good part of my afternoon stuck in traffic."

"Aw, I'm sorry to hear you're having a bad day. I wish I could be there with you and keep you company." Emma paused. "Do you really think I shouldn't go out with Evan? I don't know what happened between you and his brother, but if you think so ..."

The voice coming over the speakerphone was almost too soft to hear. The disappointment in her sister's tone tugged at her heart. Emma wasn't one to argue with anyone; she didn't have a mean bone in her body. She was as meek as they came, which was why Abby always watched out for her. With Emma hundreds of miles away on her own, she wanted to protect her even more. "It's a different ball game where you're at. People don't play nice in Hollywood. You need to be careful about who you hang out with, especially when it comes to guys. Remember what happened to me when I dated an actor? I found out how self-centered and heartless they all are. All they care about is getting ahead and leaving us little people behind."

"But I don't think Evan's like that."

"Don't be so sure. What do you really know about him other than the fact that he's hot? Didn't he date, then dump that actress from the other show? You don't need that kind of drama in your life."

"Evan never dated her. It was all made up by the tabloids. Yes, he's hot, but he's more than that. He's so sweet. He goes to a Christian actor's fellowship, and he's going to take me next time."

"Oh yeah? He's a Christian?"

"His whole family is. He's gone to church his whole life."

"Humph." Abby thought back to the questions Aiden had thrown out at the beginning of their date. He hadn't sounded so sure about his faith. But doubt was normal. She had doubted God —everything from His existence to His love for her—for the longest time until she couldn't deny it anymore. Maybe Aiden was going through a bit of that, too. Not that his spiritual state should change what she thought of him. Grr. How had he crept into her head again?

The traffic inched forward, allowing Abby to maneuver her car in and out of the lanes to reach the freeway entrance. Once she was on the highway, she let out a loud cry of relief. "Yes, I'm finally moving."

"That's great. I hope you have a smooth drive the rest of the way."

"Thanks. I hope so, too." She glanced at the photo displayed on her phone screen. The little girl who used to wear her hair in pigtails had grown up so much. There was no denying Emma was a beautiful woman now at twenty-four. A beautiful woman who could get into some serious trouble with the wrong guy. Abby felt the hair on her arms stand up at the thought of anyone mistreating her baby sister. She needed to stop this relationship before it started. "Listen Emma, I don't want to see you get hurt. Promise me you won't go out with Evan. His family is bad news."

"I-I already told him I would. I can't back out now. It would be rude of me."

Abby rolled her eyes. "He'll get over it. He's a TV star, for crying out loud. I'm sure he's got girls lined up out the door waiting to date him."

"That's the thing, Abby, he asked *me* out. He wants to go out with *me*. Isn't it crazy? And I want to go out with him."

Aside from her decision to pursue acting, she'd never heard Emma be so adamant about something before. Yikes. This was not a good sign. If she went after Evan the same way she went after her acting gigs, there was no telling what she'd do. "Emma, I'm your big sister, and as your big sister, I am warning you to stay away from Evan Spark. Don't let his good looks and charisma blind you. Celebrities all know what to say to win you over. Don't forget he's an actor. How do you know he's not pretending to like you?"

There was only silence for a moment, and Abby wondered if

the call had dropped. Traffic had slowed down again, so she took the opportunity to peek at her phone screen. What she saw made her stomach drop. Emma's pale complexion was now a ruddy color, and tears trailed down her cheeks. Abby knew that look. It was the same one she'd had the day their father left. Emma wasn't one to talk back and express her feelings. Instead, she kept them bottled up inside like a bomb waiting to explode. She hated seeing her sister like this. How could she convince her this was all for her best? "Em, I love you. You know that, right?"

All she got in response was a soft sniffle.

Keeping her eyes trained on the road, Abby tried to engage her sister in conversation. "Remember the guy you liked in high school? The one on the football team?"

"Yes."

"Remember how we all thought he was this great guy when he asked you to the Homecoming dance, but then he spent the whole evening dancing with your best friend?"

"Former best friend."

"Yes, former best friend." She winced, regretting the fact that she was bringing up Emma's past hurts. Desperate times, however, called for desperate measures. "That's the thing, Em. You're so kind and trusting, it's easy for people to take advantage of you. You gotta be more careful—suspicious, even—about who you trust. Do you understand what I'm saying?"

"I know. I made some bad choices in friends when I was younger." She hesitated. "But I'm older now. I've learned from my mistakes. I-I—" her voice wavered "—app ... pre ... ciate you looking out for me, but I n-need to make my own decisions."

Abby shook her head, not believing the words coming out of Emma's mouth. Of all the times for her sister to grow a backbone, it had to be now? Where was the obedient girl she'd known all her life?

Before Abby could get over her shock, she heard the high-pitched screeching of tires. The SUV ahead of her suddenly loomed in her line of vision. She switched her foot from the gas to the brake and stepped down, but not before a loud *bang* filled the inside of the car. A great force punched her chest and face. White powder flew everywhere, making it hard to breathe. The last thing she remembered before blacking out was hearing her sister scream.

Chapter Thirteen

AIDEN

The day had turned out better than Aiden had expected. After a lecture on women's suffrage and back-to-back office hour appointments, he was tired but satisfied. He felt most alive when he engaged with students and saw their faces light up about the course material. It was the closest thing to what he'd experienced—and still craved—on stage during a performance, the interaction between him and his fans. Although, admittedly, his students weren't as wild about him as his fans were, but the female ones still had a spark in their eyes when they saw him. It was a nice feeling to be held in such high regard, especially by young people.

Times had changed since he was a pop star. Social media held everyone's attention and it was a challenge to compete with the culture's fast pace. He shook his head as he cleaned up his desk and gathered up his belongings. It was a good thing he'd made it big when he had; he wouldn't be able to survive as a singer these days.

The thought made him chuckle. There was talk going around online about a former boy band reuniting. Aiden didn't understand why anyone in their thirties would want to go back to that kind of lifestyle—the packed schedules, all those days on the road, being chased by the paparazzi—unless they needed the money. Even then, there was no guarantee of success. The only reason he'd consider it would be for the pure joy of performing for others. There was no emotional high like it. He did miss it, but did he miss it enough?

He pushed those crazy notions out of his mind, locked up his office, and started toward the parking lot. The afternoon sun was extra powerful, thanks to a mid-September heat wave. These Indian summers were common in California, and he usually survived them in the air-conditioned buildings on campus. He thought about going home, but the silence of an empty house didn't seem so appealing. Instead, he decided to visit his brother Colin.

The middle child of the family, Colin was the easygoing one and somewhat of a dreamer. He had dreams and he went after them, often without much planning or foresight. Aiden often funded these ventures, including the current one of an ice cream shop in downtown Palo Alto. He drove the ten minutes to the store and pulled into a parking spot on the street. From his car, he saw a crowd of children and their mothers enjoying their cold treats. Business had picked up, thanks to the weather. For once, it seemed one of Colin's ideas was panning out.

Aiden entered the shop and waved to the dark-haired man behind the counter. Both hands holding ice cream cones, his brother nodded in greeting. He handed off the cones to some pint-sized customers and strode over to Aiden's table with a big grin.

"Hey, boss! I didn't expect to see you today." Colin grabbed him in a tight bear hug, lifting him off the floor for a moment. He'd been a linebacker in college and had his sights on going pro before a knee injury changed his plans. The setback hadn't affected his attitude though. "Do you want your usual? How about two scoops today? It's a great day. The sun's out, the shop's full, life is grand!"

"What's gotten into you?" Aiden eyed his brother with curiosity. "Why are you so happy?"

"Can't a guy be happy?"

"Yes. But this—" he pointed to Colin's face and drew a circle with his finger "—is not normal, even for you."

Colin shrugged and glanced around the brightly-lit shop. Pops of color—every hue from bright reds to blues to yellows—surrounded them in every aspect of the decor. Even the plastic spoons the customers used were colored. "Look around, bro. I'm surrounded by happy things and happy people. And lots of sugar. You can't not be happy here. I'm glad you showed up. You could use a little cheer of your own." He playfully punched Aiden in the shoulder. "So, I heard through the Spark-line you went on a date. That's great news, bro. How was it?"

If Colin expected him to exude happiness, that was the wrong topic to bring up. Aiden set his jaw and drawled, "It was horrible. The worst date ever."

"The worst? The worst would be if she didn't show up. She didn't do that, did she?"

He wished Abby *had* stood him up. Then she wouldn't have targeted him with her derogatory remarks. How dare she accuse him of not caring about people? Maybe he could do more for the community, but it would mean going back into the public eye, something he wasn't ready for. He had valid reasons for his actions—or non-actions—and he didn't need to justify himself to anyone, especially not to that woman. "I don't want to think about it, much less talk about it. I hope I never see her again."

Colin's eyes grew wide and he slowly took a few steps back. "All righty then. No talking about the date. I'll go get your ice cream. Be right back."

Aiden watched his brother scoop a generous helping of vanilla into a chocolate-dipped waffle cone. Then another scoop.

On top of the sugar monstrosity, he added some sprinkles, chopped walnuts, and whipped cream. Colin held up his creation with a beaming smile. Aiden offered a smile in return. There was no way he'd ever eat that much sugar in one go, but seeing his brother happy made him happy. Colin's attitude was contagious.

"Here you are. You might want to use a spoon." Colin handed him the cone, along with a spoon and napkin. "I gotta go man the counter. The college kid who was supposed to come in today called in sick. I'll check back on you in a bit. Shout if you need anything."

"Thanks." Aiden took out his phone to check his emails, then swiped open the browser to check the news. He bypassed the political and sports headlines until he reached the entertainment section. Even though he was no longer in the business, he still liked to stay up-to-date on the latest music.

In between licks of his ice cream, he learned which bands were on the charts and which artists were now guest judges on a reality singing show. He intentionally scrolled past the celebrity news, but stopped when a familiar face popped up on his screen. One week of not checking their family's group chat room and he'd missed some important news. He looked up and caught Colin's attention. "Did you know about this?"

Colin squinted at Aiden's phone as he neared. "Oh yeah, Evan met a girl on set this week. Gorgeous redhead. She's from the Bay Area, too, and a believer. She might be playing his girlfriend on the show."

"Is that all?" Their youngest brother was a responsible kid, which made news about him so much more infuriating to read. The rumors swirling about him on the internet changed from day to day, making him sound fickle and immature. Today's headline said it all: *Evan Spark dumps girlfriend; spotted with new love!* "Why can't they get the facts straight? He never even went out with that actress. They were spotted in the same restaurant one night, and everyone started making assumptions. And now this? They make it sound like he's in love."

"Oh, it's not too far off. He really likes this girl. I've never heard him talk about anyone like this before."

"We'll see about that," Aiden scoffed. "Nothing's real in Hollywood. Who knows, she's probably using him to get her name out there."

Colin winced. "You should eat more of that ice cream."

Aiden smirked as he noticed a puddle forming on the table. Great. The cone had a leak. Even his ice cream reminded him of how messy life was. He tossed it into a nearby trash can and wiped his hands. His phone vibrated on the table with an incoming call, displaying Evan's face on the screen. What great timing. At least he could talk some sense into his brother.

"Hey, Evan. I'm glad you called."

"Aiden, I need your help! Emma's sister's been in a car accident. She can't reach her, but she said you'd know how to. Can you help? She's worried sick—"

"What? What are you talking about? Who's Emma?" Aiden mouthed the last question again to Colin who was eyeing him curiously.

"The girl he likes!" Colin murmured before reaching into the back pocket of his jeans. His phone was ringing as well. "Hello?"

"Aiden, are you listening?" The urgency in Evan's voice brought his focus back to the phone call. "Can you get in touch with Abby Dearan and see if she's okay?"

Abby? The only Abby he knew was that insufferable deejay, the woman who demanded he pay for the meal *she* ate. Why was Evan asking him about her? "I have no idea where Abby is. I only have her phone number."

"Yo, Aiden, can you man the shop for me?" Colin's voice boomed in his other ear. "Candy got rear-ended on 101 South. She needs me to pick her up."

When had Colin become Candy's personal driver? Aiden

blinked and saw his brother waving impatiently at him. He nodded. "Sure, I'll stay here. You go."

"Come on, Aiden," Evan urged in his other ear. "Emma's frantic. She was on the phone with her sister when the airbag went off. She was driving home on 101 South. Can you call around to the nearby hospitals? Anything you can do will help."

Aiden shook his head, his thoughts clashing together like a dissonant chord. How was it possible Evan was interested in Abby's sister? And what were the chances both Abby and Candy got into car accidents around the same time, on the same highway? An airbag might as well have punched *him* in the face. His sensed his worlds colliding, and he was in the middle of it all.

Chapter Fourteen

ABBY

*A*bby woke up to the wail of a siren in the distance. Eyes closed, she heard it grow louder and louder, signaling a fast approach. The sound blared in her ears until it suddenly stopped. After a minute, she heard frantic knocking on her driver's side window. The knocking competed with the throbbing in her head, making her groan. Who was making all that racket and why wouldn't they leave her alone? She just wanted to go back to sleep.

"Miss, can you hear me?" A male voice called out to her. "Can you open the door?"

Huh? What door? And why did her lips feel like they were coated with powdered sugar from a donut? She opened her mouth to ask the man what was going on but gagged at the bitter taste on her tongue. Grimacing, she lifted her lashes and spotted a puffy white cushion against her torso. That's when she remembered—she'd rammed into the car in front of her. Oh, could her day get any worse? But, she reasoned with herself, she was still alive and well, even if her car wasn't. That was reason enough to thank God ... before she asked for His help. She most certainly needed some divine intervention.

Abby turned to her left and spotted a man dressed in a dark uniform. She assumed from the bright yellow helmet on his head he was a firefighter. At his urging, she unlocked the door and pushed it open. Her lungs welcomed the air outside even though it was laced with exhaust fumes. She squeezed past the airbag and practically fell into his arms. The shock of what had happened suddenly hit her. Hot tears welled in her eyes as she clung onto him.

"You're safe now, Miss. Let's get you checked out."

She squinted, suddenly realizing how blurry the scene appeared. She must've lost her glasses when the airbag exploded. Leaning on the firefighter for support, Abby let him lead her to the side of the highway where two ambulances, along with a fire truck, were parked. Several police officers were on hand, placing flares on the ground and directing traffic. She noticed a couple of vehicles lined up in front of and behind her car, their bumpers all damaged. Obviously, there had been a domino effect at play, which meant she likely wasn't the one to blame for the accident. The thought gave her some comfort. At least her insurance premium wouldn't increase.

Near the side of the fire truck, the firefighter handed Abby off to his colleague in a similar-looking uniform. "This is Lieutenant Spark. You'll be in good hands with him."

"Hello, Miss." The tall young man greeted her with a smile, then gasped. "I'm sorry, what did you say your name was?"

Abby grimaced. Maybe she looked as horrible as she felt. "What is it? Do I look bad?"

"No, not at all. Please have a seat." He stared at her for an extra beat before helping her onto the stretcher which extended from the side of the truck. "Your name, please?"

"It's Abby. Abby Dearan."

"If you don't mind, Abby, I'm going to check your vitals."

After a thorough assessment, he determined she should be taken to the emergency room as a precaution since her airbag had deployed. Despite her protests, Abby soon found herself inside an ambulance wearing a neck brace while strapped to a backboard. Talk about unpleasant. What she wouldn't give to have a soft mattress to lie on, anything besides this hard, cold plastic.

"Is there someone I can call for you?" The firefighter eyed her with concern. "A family member or friend?"

"Emma!" Abby couldn't believe she'd forgotten about her sister. She must have freaked out when their call was cut short. "My phone's in the car. Can you get it for me? I need to call my sister and let her know I'm okay."

"Sure. You stay put. I'll be right back."

Abby moved the only part of herself that was still mobile—her eyes—and rolled them. Like she could go anywhere even if she wanted to. She watched the man walk away, then stared up at the ceiling of the ambulance.

She got to wondering how the other drivers had fared. Were any of them seriously hurt? If she needed this much attention for some non-existent injuries, she hoped no one else did, too. She said a quick prayer for the other folks, just as she heard someone approaching. A police officer hopped inside the ambulance and flashed a badge at her.

The officer proceeded to ask some routine questions about what had happened, as well as the extent of her injuries. Abby answered her to the best of her abilities, but she honestly didn't remember much of the accident. She hoped the other drivers had a better recollection.

Soon after, the firefighter returned with her phone. He held it up for her to see. Darn. The screen was cracked, and she had a hard time deciphering the new texts on the screen. As she debated what to do, she heard a young woman's voice echo inside the ambulance.

"Darren! Fancy meeting you here."

"Candy? Was that your car near the back? No wonder it looked familiar. Are you hurt?"

"Some minor bruising, but I'm fine. I wanted to see how this driver's doing. I was in the car behind theirs. Is he or she going to be okay?"

"Funny you should ask about her." The firefighter's face hovered above Abby's as he asked, "Do you feel well enough to see someone?"

"I guess so."

"Go ahead, Candy. But you might need to sit down afterwards," he cautioned her before stepping away.

A woman in her early thirties appeared at Abby's side. Her face was perfectly made up and she wore small gold hoop earrings to complement a bold statement necklace. Not a strand of hair was out of place. For someone who'd been in a car accident, she looked way too gorgeous and put-together. Abby bet she'd make even a neck brace look chic.

The woman took one look at Abby, and her jaw went slack. She reached out to touch her face. Her voice wavered as she whispered, "Mandy?"

"You have the wrong person. My name's Abby."

The woman blinked quickly, her eyes moist with unshed tears. She shook her head and released a heavy breath. "I-I'm sorry. You look so much like my sister. Or how I think she would look if— never mind." She paused. "How are you feeling? I think you got the brunt of the impact from being in the middle of all the cars."

"I didn't even know I got hit from the back. I blacked out when the airbag went off. I'm sure I'll be fine. This getup is all a precaution."

"I'm so glad you're okay." She gestured over her shoulder. "None of the other drivers were seriously hurt either. They complained about some bruising and soreness, but no broken bones. God had His angels working overtime today. It could've been a lot worse."

Abby grunted in agreement.

"Is there anything I can do for you? Does your family know you're okay?"

"Actually, would you call my sister? My phone's out of commission."

"Sure thing." She took a phone out of her jacket pocket and swiped it open. "What's her number?"

Abby relayed the information to her. "Thank you. It's Candy, right?"

"Yes, and you're very welcome." She dialed Emma's number and waited. "Hi Emma? I have you sister, Abby, here. She wants to talk to you."

Candy positioned the phone next to Abby's ear. She winced when the sound of her sister's high-pitched cry came over the line. "Em, calm down. I'm okay, more than okay."

"I was so worried, Abby. When the call dropped, I started freaking out. I didn't know what to do, so I asked Evan to call his brother. I thought maybe he'd know where you were."

Abby couldn't believe her ears. "Emma, you did what? Why would you reach out to Aiden Spark after I specifically told you I didn't like the guy?" How strange. She thought she felt Candy's hand flinch at the mention of Aiden, or perhaps the phone had slipped from her hand.

"I know, I know," Emma answered in a regretful tone. "I wasn't thinking straight. I thought since Aiden lives near you, he could find you for me. He said he'd call around to the local hospitals and check."

"He did? That's surprising." The thought that Aiden still cared enough to help her sister tugged at her heart. Then again, he was more than likely doing the favor for his brother.

Emma mumbled something to someone on her end. After a moment, she returned to speak with Abby. "Evan's going to let his brother know you're okay."

The firefighter returned to Abby's left side with a clipboard in his hands. He gestured for her to finish the call. "I gotta go, Em. They're taking me to the hospital to have me checked out."

"Which hospital, Abby? I can have Evan tell his brother to meet you there."

"Emma! How many times do I have to tell you." She lowered her voice. "I don't want to see or hear from him again. I'll be fine. I need to go. I'll call you when I'm done. Love you."

"Love you, too, sis!"

Abby acknowledged Candy's questioning glance with a tight smile. "I'm done, thanks."

"Is everything okay?" Candy raised one perfectly groomed brow. She slipped her phone into her pocket and remarked, "You sounded upset. Something to do with a guy?"

"Uh ..."

"I didn't mean to eavesdrop, but I heard you say the name Aiden Spark." Candy glanced at the firefighter before returning her attention to Abby. "We happen to know someone by that name. I was wondering if it might be the same person."

Abby eyed the woman for a good five seconds. She didn't know anything about Candy other than her name and the fact that she was nosy, but she preferred it this way. Anyone with a connection to a man named Aiden was not a friend of hers. It didn't matter if Candy was referring to her Aiden or not—not that he would ever be *her* Aiden. She had more important matters to take care of, namely her health and her car. She'd need a different mode of transportation tomorrow, assuming the doctor would allow her to go in to the office. All these factors were more important than a certain professor.

She was about to tell Candy this, though not in so many words, when someone approached the ambulance.

"Candy?" a man called out. "Are you in there?"

The firefighter gestured for him to climb inside. "Colin, what are you doing here?"

"Darren, hey! Candy called me. If I'd known you were here, I wouldn't have worried so much."

Abby's eyes flitted around the small space as she took in the conversation around her. It sounded like these three were all connected in some way.

Colin rushed over and greeted Candy with a tight embrace. "There you are! I've been looking all over for you. Are you hurt?"

"I'm fine." Candy extracted herself from his arms and smoothed her hair back into place. "You didn't have to come. I only called to tell you I was running late. Who's manning the shop?"

"Of course I came. You're more important to me than work. Don't sweat it, Aiden's there."

Candy seemed to soften at Colin's words. Abby admitted, even she melted a little. Now, this was the way to treat a woman. Candy was one lucky girl. Abby diverted her gaze so as not to intrude on the couple's intimate moment. The act was pointless, however, because Candy brought her right into the conversation with her next remark.

"Colin, this is Abby. She was in the car in front of me. I'm really glad I bumped into her today." One side of her mouth lifted in a half-smile. "Not literally, of course."

"Hi Abby, I'm sorry to meet you under these circumstances." The man's voice boomed loudly within the ambulance. "I hope you have a fast recovery."

Abby tried her best to look to the right without turning her head. She locked gazes with Colin out of the corner of her eye. She was speechless. Not only was he good-looking, he was considerate, too. Why couldn't she meet a guy like him?

Colin seemed speechless as well. He stared at her as if she were a ghost. He looked from Abby to Candy, then back again, still in disbelief.

What was it with everyone today? Abby wrinkled her nose.

She must have a doppelganger out there, someone very loved by these three people. "If you were wondering, I'm not Mandy."

Colin released a deep breath and shook his head. "How is this possible?"

"That was my reaction, too, when I first saw her," Darren piped up. "I apologize if I stared earlier," he confessed to Abby. "I was caught off guard. I never expected to see her—I mean, you."

"No worries," she replied, still unsure of what was going on. "I must really look like this Mandy person."

"You're a spitting image of her," Colin agreed, "of what she'd look like if she were still alive."

Still alive? Abby swallowed. This Mandy wasn't around anymore. No wonder they were so fascinated with her. "I'm so sorry for your loss. I hope it's not weird seeing me like this."

"Not weird at all." Candy's smile was bittersweet. "Seeing you makes me feel closer to my sister, closer than I've felt in a long time."

"You know who else needs to see her?" Colin murmured to Candy.

She nodded knowingly. "It might help. Maybe he'll get the closure he needs, once and for all."

Okay, now Abby was the nosy one. Who were they talking about? Was it possible she could help someone by being her plain 'ol self? She had to find out. "If there's something I can do to help, just let me know."

Candy exchanged hopeful glances with the two men. "Really? That would be awesome. What do you think, guys?"

"It's worth a try," Darren answered.

"Definitely." Colin grinned at Abby and asked, "Would it be okay if we arranged for our brother to meet you? Mandy was his girlfriend. He's had a rough time since she passed away."

"Oh, I'm sorry to hear that. Of course, if you think it would help him." Abby chewed on her lower lip as she thought. She'd heard that God works in mysterious ways, but this was unlike anything she'd ever imagined. "Maybe some good will come out of this accident. I'd be happy to meet him."

"Thank you. I'm sure Aiden will appreciate it."

Wait, what was it about that name? Why did she keep hearing it today? "Aiden?"

"Yeah, our brother's name is Aiden. Aiden Spark."

No. Freaking. Way. Why couldn't she get away from that man? She had no idea what God was up to, but she had a feeling it was something big.

Chapter Fifteen

AIDEN

*A*iden took shallow breaths as he glanced around the hospital waiting room. He had wanted to escape the moment those familiar antiseptic odors assaulted his senses. The sight of people in scrubs made his stomach turn, bringing him back to the days he'd kept vigil by Mandy's side. Waiting and praying, praying and waiting for God to answer his prayers. Being surrounded by everything he'd tried to avoid the past decade made his heart race. Cold beads of sweat broke out along his temple as he hunched over in his chair. This was the last place he wanted to be.

Why had he agreed to drive Candy over to see Abby? Why did Colin have to do inventory at the store tonight of all nights? Why couldn't he have escaped to the solace of his home? Well, he knew why. It was the niggling feeling in the back of his mind that he couldn't shake ever since Colin and Candy had confronted him about knowing Abby. Call it conviction ... or curiosity? There did seem to be too many coincidences for it to be random. Even if he didn't feel like speaking to God, he had to acknowledge His hand at work. Just what was He up to? And why did this woman keep popping up in his life?

He admitted guilt played a factor, too. He'd been a jerk to Abby. No woman deserved to be treated the way he'd treated her. He thought about telling her this in person here, but maybe he'd do it over the phone later. The sooner he left the hospital, the better. He needed to leave this place and all his dreaded memories with it.

"Aiden?"

A hand touched his shoulder. He lifted his head to find Candy looking at him in concern. His mouth dry, he whispered, "Are you done? Can we go?"

She crouched down next to him. "Hey, talk to me. What's going on?"

The gentleness in her tone surprised him. He was used to Candy's assertive, demanding side, but this was new. He took it as a sign he must look bad, as bad as he felt. His hands and fingers tingled and grew numb, but he forced them to grip the wooden armrests. He steadied himself as the room began to spin. "I h-hate being here."

Understanding registered in her eyes. "I know. I don't like it either. But no one's dying today. Abby's fine. All her tests came back clear. She's waiting to be discharged. I told her we'd take her home. She doesn't have anyone who can pick her up."

Great. So, he would get to apologize to her in person, if he survived the wait. It was getting harder to sit still. His stomach churned with each passing second. Eyes squeezed shut, Aiden could only nod.

Candy took the seat next to his. Her voice was firm again, and one high-heeled shoe tapped out an impatient rhythm on the tile floor. "I appreciate you driving me. I can't believe your brother said I wasn't allowed to take my car anywhere until I got it checked out. Doesn't he know I have places to go? Who does he think I am?"

Candy's tirade grew muffled as if she'd moved across the room. Aiden opened his eyes to see where she'd gone, but he only saw a haze of colors. The room closed in on him. He opened his mouth to draw in some air, but the heavy sensation crushing his chest made it next to impossible. Was this what it felt like to die? Because he was sure he was going to meet his Maker ... and the only thing he could think about was how disappointed God would be to see him. Regret and fear held him hostage as the world darkened around him, and he slumped to the ground.

"Lord, please help Aiden."

Whose voice was that? Aiden wondered if his radio alarm had gone off because the woman talking had a clear and bright voice made for the radio.

"I know You like him a lot more than I do," the voice continued, "so I'm asking You to wake him up. Please let him be okay."

Aiden stirred slowly in his bed, feeling like he'd finally gotten a full night of sleep. His body seemed rested, but oh, his head was pounding. He raised one hand to his forehead and came upon a lump. What had happened?

"Hey! You're awake," the woman exclaimed. "Thank God. It's a nasty bump, but the rest of your face is still gorge—good."

Was she about to say gorgeous? Aiden opened his eyes and came face-to-face with a gorgeous vision in her own right. Abby looked the way he remembered, minus the piece of spinach between her teeth.

His gaze drifted to the white sterile wall behind her, jump-starting his memories. That's right—he'd blacked out in the waiting room. He propped himself up on his elbows and realized he was now lying on a hospital bed. Grimacing, he muttered, "This is embarrassing."

She leaned back, suddenly startled. "The doctor said you had a panic attack. Candy's on the phone with your brother, Colin." She glanced over her shoulder into the hall, then back at him. "How are you feeling?"

"Okay. Better." He sat up and ran one hand down his face. It felt strange to be having a normal conversation with Abby after how their last exchange had gone down. How was she so calm ... and nice? He wouldn't have blamed her if she never spoke to him again. "Uh, how are you? I mean, with the accident?"

"I'm fine. I'm just thankful to be alive. Getting punched with an airbag really helps knock some sense into you about what's important in life." She squinted as she looked at him. "Sorry if it looks like I'm staring. I can't see without my glasses. They broke during the crash."

Aiden noticed some slight bruising around the bridge of her nose. "That must've hurt."

"Yeah, but I'd rather it be my glasses than my nose." She shifted nervously on her feet. "Well, I guess it wouldn't matter either way. That's why I'm in the line of work I'm in. I have a face fit for radio."

The chuckle she added didn't fool him. Aiden sensed she wasn't comfortable in her own skin. Which was odd, considering how beautiful she was. "I think you have a beautiful voice *and* face."

"Ha!" she scoffed. She looked at him cautiously. "Is this your way of apologizing?"

"No, what? It's the truth. I mean, yes, I do want to apologize, but I didn't say it as an apology."

Abby shook her head. "Forget I brought it up. I don't care about what happened between us. Arguing seems so pointless and petty now. Being in the crash today made me realize how short and precious life is. We shouldn't waste our time dwelling on the past." Her expression sobered. "But I think you knew that already."

"Uh, yeah." Yet, he'd still couldn't shake the past.

"I heard about your girlfriend, Mandy. I'm so sorry."

"Thanks."

"Did what happened out there—" she gestured toward the waiting room "—have something to do with her?"

He released a deep breath. He never talked about what had happened with Mandy or the band. But maybe it was time he did. "This is the hospital where she died."

She winced. "I had no idea. The news never even mentioned you were dating someone."

"That's because I did everything I could to keep her out of the spotlight. She didn't sign up for that life; I did. I tried to protect her as much as I could." He swallowed hard. There were some things he couldn't save her from.

"Is she the reason you left Heartland?"

"I left the band because it wasn't right to have success without her. I didn't deserve it."

"You decided to punish yourself for her illness?"

He met her gaze. "Don't you get it? I must've done something wrong. Mandy didn't deserve to get sick and die. She wasn't the one who went after record contracts and fame. She loved God with all her heart. She loved everyone around her. Even when she was at her weakest, she was the one encouraging us, encouraging me. She had accepted her fate. I was the one praying for a miracle. I obviously didn't do something right because He took her from me."

Abby nodded slowly as if thinking through his words. "I can understand how you came to this conclusion, but it's wrong."

"Wrong?" The last thing he wanted was some deep theological

sermon. "Please don't give me some spiritual mumbo-jumbo speech about there being a lesson in all of this. I've been a Christian since I was seven; I've heard it all."

"Trust me, I'm the last person who'd give you a speech. I've only known God for a year, so I'm still learning. But the one thing I'm sure of is God loves us. Only a loving God would die for sinful people like us. 'Cause that's what it's all about, isn't it? Him making things right so we can have a relationship with Him. It sounds like Mandy understood that."

"Well, under the circumstances, she had to," he scoffed, not even attempting to hold back the bitterness in his tone. "There wasn't much else to hold onto in the end."

"She still had a choice whether or not to believe. God doesn't force us to love Him. That's not what love's about. He asks us to trust Him. Believe me, I don't trust people very easily, but everything He's done proves He's worth trusting."

He blinked in disbelief. Not only did she say all the right words, she sounded like she believed them. Good for her. He needed a healthy dose of what she had. It reminded him of Mandy's unwavering faith. Why was it so easy for some people, but not for him? "I'm glad you have it all figured out. I wish I could say the same for myself."

She gave him a small smile. "Not completely, but it's a start. It took me a good ten years before I made the jump to believe. My friend, Danica, stuck through it with me when I had my doubts. I wouldn't be where I am without her. Sometimes we need a little push in the right direction. In my case, she was the one who did the pushing."

The phrase Danica had mentioned on their date popped out of his mouth. "Iron sharpens iron."

"Yes, exactly!" Abby's face brightened. "Danica says that all the time."

He laughed wryly. "I bet she does."

Funny how the events of the past week were coming together like a well-orchestrated piece of music. Who knew one wrong text would lead him and Abby—not to mention, their siblings and friends—to this moment? How could he deny God's hand at work in his life, even amid his doubt? It was more than he wanted to deal with at the moment. He pushed the thought aside in favor of something lighter. "Uh, this is off topic, but do you happen to know if she's interested in my brother, Brandon?"

"Oh, she would kill me if I told you, but yes." Abby grinned. "Do you know how he feels? She says he's a romance author, but he doesn't seem to have a romantic bone in his body."

"Yeah, that's Brandon for you. He's a little lacking when it comes to socializing in the real world. Our family jokes he can only talk to fictional women." He laughed. "I can do some digging around and find out for you."

"I'd appreciate it. Danica's done so much for me, I'd do anything to help her."

Abby's smile was so sweet and genuine, it warmed him to the core. He found himself captivated by her face. She looked so much like Mandy, but with a unique beauty of her own. Without her glasses on, he saw flecks of gold in her light brown eyes. They matched her fiery personality, the part of her that grated on his nerves when they first met. Seeing her love for her friend, however, made him appreciate all the aspects of who she was. She had both compassion and conviction; it was a rare combination. "You really are beautiful."

Her cheeks flushed, and she raised one palm to her cheek to raise her glasses. When she realized she didn't have them on, she bit her lower lip in embarrassment. "You must've hit your head hard when you fell. You're seeing things."

"No, I'm not," he insisted with a smile. "You're as beautiful as I remember. I'm really glad to see you again, even under these less-than-ideal circumstances."

A line appeared between her brows. She dropped her head and

mumbled, "I forgot they wanted to do a CAT scan when you woke up. I'll go get the nurse."

She spun on her heels and rushed out of the exam room before Aiden could say a word. Her absence immediately made its mark, leaving him lonelier than he'd been in a long time. It was an unexpected, yet intriguing feeling.

Chapter Sixteen

ABBY

*a*bby clung onto the overhead hand grip as she stood wedged between two passengers on the BART train to San Francisco. Since the accident a couple of days ago, her car had been parked on the street corner by her apartment. It needed major repairs, repairs she couldn't afford at the present time— maybe ever. She was left to take public transportation until she scrounged up enough money. While she was thankful to be alive, the daily commute to and from work left her with sore feet and a grumpy attitude. Her only consolation? Listening to music on her phone.

She adjusted her earbuds and turned up the volume. A soft guitar intro signaled the beginning of a ballad from Heartland's greatest hits album. Soon after, a male tenor began singing about love and heartbreak. How appropriate. Hearing Aiden's voice brought comfort to her weary body, but it also left her heart aching.

She hadn't seen or spoken to him since the day at the hospital. She hadn't even said a proper goodbye, choosing to call an Uber after she left him in the exam room. It was her way of protecting herself. She didn't want to fall for a man who was in love with another woman. Because all Aiden saw when he looked at her was his old girlfriend. Why else would he have called her beautiful?

She couldn't compete with Mandy; the woman sounded like a saint. Even on her best days when she kept her mouth shut, she still thought things that were less than gracious. But that's why she loved God, because He accepted her with all her flaws. Plus, she didn't want to compete with anyone else for a man's attention. Not even for a man like Aiden Spark.

She'd already had a soft spot for him in her heart, even before she knew about his sad past. She now needed to guard her heart more than ever. Lock that baby up and throw away the key.

Abby tried not to dwell on the memory of Aiden's sweet smile as she sat down at her desk forty minutes later. She kicked off her sneakers and began prepping her notes for the day's show. She scrolled through several paparazzi sites for the latest celebrity news, trying her best to decipher which information was true and which was false. Some of the allegations were incredulous; all were demeaning. She hated to admit it, but Aiden had a point. It might be interesting and fun to talk about these rumors on the air, but nothing good came from them. God had given her such an amazing platform; she needed to find better ways to use it.

A renewed determination flowed through her veins. She did some more searches, this time for positive news stories. There had to be a celebrity or two who went out of their way to help people. It took a couple of tries, but she finally found some news-worthy talking points. One band had given a special concert to benefit the victims of a recent hurricane. Another pop artist had visited a fan recovering from surgery. Abby smiled as she read each story. Now this was the kind of news she could get behind.

"What are you so happy about?"

She'd been so involved in her research, she hadn't heard Marcus walk into the studio. The confused look on his face made her laugh. "Can't a girl be happy?"

"Yes, but not the one I work with." He approached his chair

slowly as if walking around land mines. "Who are you and what have you done with my coworker?"

Abby rolled her eyes. "It's me, Marcus. I know I've been a little hard to work with lately." At the sight of his raised brows, she corrected herself. "Okay, I've been really hard to work with, but I've found the answer to my problems. Some of my problems." Her love life was a different and utterly hopeless matter.

"What is it? You found the solution to world peace?"

"Close." She pointed at her computer screen. "Let's forget the rumors and gossip and instead talk about how celebrities are making a positive impact on the world. We can even encourage our listeners to find their own ways to help people. It doesn't have to be anything major, just little things they can do to pay it forward. Buy coffee for a stranger, offer to mow a neighbor's lawn —the list is endless. This could turn into something big, something great." Excitement hummed through her body from her head to her toes. She could hardly sit still, she was almost giddy.

"Whoa, okay, now I'm really scared. Who are you?" Marcus stared at her as if she'd grown another head. "I don't know what you did with Abby Dearan, but I don't care. I like this new Abby. She's a much better improvement over the cynical, mopey—ouch!"

She cut him off with a playful punch to the arm. "You were saying?"

He pretended to cower in fear as he nursed his arm. "Yep, it's still you in there."

"Be serious. What do you think of my idea?"

He nodded thoughtfully. "It's different, but good. I think it'll work well, especially with the holidays coming up. It's a good time to get people thinking about helping others."

She grinned. "It's always a good time to help others."

Marcus studied her for a beat before asking, "What made you want to do this?"

"Honestly? It was something Aiden Spark said."

"Aiden Spark? I didn't think I'd hear you say his name ever again."

"Yeah, well, that was the final time." She turned her chair to face her monitor, ending the conversation. It was still a sore subject, one she didn't want Marcus meddling in. "Enough chit-chat. We're on the air in twenty."

Four hours later, the phones in the studio were still ringing off the hook. Their producer gave them two thumbs-up through the glass partition, along with a big smile. The response to the "Play It Forward" campaign, as she and Marcus had come to call it, was a huge hit with their listeners. For every tenth caller who shared a story of how they helped someone, they were given the chance to request a song. The station also shared the request on social media and tagged the song's artist and asked them to pay it forward as well. The campaign was already a trending topic, making it a win-win for everyone involved.

Abby was in awe that a single idea had sparked an entire movement. She took a moment to close her eyes and give thanks to God. Despite all her imperfections, He was still using her. It was a humbling thought.

"Hey, we've got the next winner on the line. Do you want to take it?"

She opened her eyes at Marcus's prompting. "Sure," she answered him as she pressed the button to take the call. "Hi there, Abby here. Guess what, you're caller ten!"

A breathless female voice shrieked in excitement. "I am? I can't believe it!"

"Yes, you are. Why don't you tell us your name and your story?"

"I'm Bria. I've been helping a friend who's blind by recording myself reading her favorite author's books to her. I read them chapter by chapter and upload the videos to YouTube."

"That's so cool, Bria. You sound like an awesome friend. So, what song would you like to request?"

"Is an old song okay? There's a band I loved back in the day. They're not together anymore, but I sometimes hear you guys play their songs."

"Sure, go for it."

"It's Heartland's *See You Again*. I love the lead singer's voice. Is there any way you can tag Aiden Spark or the band? I don't even know if they have any social media accounts."

Abby gulped. The mere mention of Aiden's name made her heart race. "I don't know, but I'll check. I'm a big fan of his, too." In more ways than one, she hated to admit. "Thanks for calling in, Bria, and playing it forward. Listen for your request coming up next."

She switched off her mic and cued up the next song. When she glanced up from her computer, she saw Marcus looking at her curiously. A little too curiously. "Yes? I know you want to say something, so say it."

He shrugged. "I was wondering how you plan on getting in touch with Aiden Spark. I'm pretty sure he doesn't have any online presence, aside from his mysterious faculty profile."

"He's gotta have something. Everyone has a virtual footprint. I'll try Twitter or Instagram. Or maybe Myspace."

"Okay, but what if he doesn't exist online? How are you going to let him know about the campaign then?"

"I'll worry about it when we get to that point—" she narrowed her eyes "—*if* we get to that point."

He wiped the grin off his face and ducked his head.

Abby rolled her eyes. What was Marcus trying to imply? If she didn't find him online, she'd have to reach out to him personally? That was not gonna happen ... right?

Wrong.

Half an hour and a dozen web searches later, she had no leads whatsoever. Aiden Spark was nowhere to be found online. How he'd managed to stay off social media was nothing short of a miracle. Especially for a celebrity—or former celebrity as he liked to insist.

Abby sat back in her chair and groaned. "Okay, you win," she muttered to Marcus. "I can't find him anywhere. What am I supposed to do now?"

Marcus shot her a smug smile. "You have the guy's number, don't you?"

"I am not calling Aiden Spark."

"Text him then."

She glared at him. "No. Freaking. Way. That's how this whole craziness started, remember?"

"But what about Bria and her good deed? Shouldn't you help her pay it forward? You did promise you'd find Aiden for her."

"I hardly promised anything, Marcus. And stop trying to make me feel guilty."

"It's your conscience talking, not me," he added with a wink.

He could call it whatever he wanted because Abby was not going to give in to the urge to pick up her phone. She didn't miss him. Nope, the only reason she'd contact Aiden Spark was to spread goodness. It was all for a worthy cause. That's what she told herself hours later when she dialed his number.

Chapter Seventeen
AIDEN

*A*iden opened his front door and ushered Brandon inside. He spotted the bag of Chinese take-out in his hands. His mouth watered at the savory smells wafting in the air between them. "You brought dinner? You're the best. Thanks, Bran."

Brandon eyed him curiously. "I always bring dinner."

He took the bag from his brother and set the white cartons on the large dining table. Not bothering to grab a plate, he began picking at each one of them. He stopped eating—his wooden chopsticks halfway to his mouth—when he realized Brandon was staring at him. "Do you want some of this before I eat it all? I'm starving."

"I can see that. No worries, I'll take the fried rice." He took a seat across from Aiden, an amused grin lighting up his eyes. He grabbed some chopsticks as well and took a box of for himself. "I'm glad your appetite's back. I haven't seen you this hungry in a long time."

Aiden swallowed a hearty mouthful of chow mein. "Writing always makes me hungry. Must be all the brain cells I burn coming up with a melody."

Brandon's head whipped up at Aiden's words. "You're writing a song?" His question came out cautiously but tinged with excitement.

"Ever since I got home. The chorus came to me as I was driving and I got two verses down so far. I'm working on the bridge now." He chewed his food as quickly as possible and washed it down with a glass of water. His fingers itched to get back to his guitar. He had forgotten Brandon was coming over for his usual Wednesday night dinner until the doorbell rang. His earlier annoyance at being interrupted disappeared as soon as he saw his brother had brought food over. At least now he'd have the sustenance to continue his songwriting.

"That's fantastic, bro. I'm so happy for you."

"It feels good to have the creative juices flowing again. What doesn't feel good are my fingers." Aiden held up the reddened fingertips of his left hand. "These are not guitar-friendly right now. But they will be soon enough. Give me ten days and I'll have my calluses back."

"Do you hear yourself?" Brandon smiled as he set his carton down. "The old Aiden is back. You're back, man."

"You're calling me old?" Aiden quipped. "Need I remind you we'll be the same age in a month?"

"You know what I'm talking about. I meant the old Aiden, as in the pop star Aiden, is back."

He shook his head. "Don't say that. I'm never going back to being that guy. I'm writing this song for myself and for myself only."

Brandon shrugged. "I don't care who you write it for as long as you keep writing." He paused, thoughtfully. "You're a different person when you write. I've missed that guy."

"Different?" It had been so long since he'd picked up a guitar, much less written a song, he didn't remember that part of himself. But Brandon obviously did. "Different how?"

"It's like you have a sense of purpose. There's an energy about you that comes from deep inside. You're happy, man."

He smirked. His brother made it sound like he hadn't been happy before today. Well, there was some truth to that statement. Okay, there was a lot of truth to it. It'd been a long time since he'd felt excited about anything, especially music. Music had been his enemy for the past decade, but today it felt like the blood rushing through his veins, giving him life. "It's been a while since I felt a drive to create. I had the worst writer's block for a very long time."

"I know what that's like," Brandon mused. "It's the hardest thing to get back into the groove. That's when you need a muse to jump start your inspiration. It looks like you found yours."

Aiden took the opportunity to stuff his mouth full to the point where it made talking impossible. His brother's tone suggested there was more to his words than he was letting on, and he wasn't sure he wanted to address the issue. Or the person at the heart of the issue: Abby.

It'd been a couple of days since she had left the hospital without so much as a goodbye. Maybe she hadn't gotten over the way he'd mistreated her. Maybe she didn't want anything more to do with him. Either possibility made his heart ache, and it was regret and longing that drove him to write. She was possibly the worst muse he'd ever had. He couldn't get her off his mind, and it was driving him crazy. Crazy to the point where he'd started praying again, if only to vent his frustrations to God. On second thought, she had to be his best muse to get him to open up his heart again.

Brandon opened another carton of food and ate an egg roll before he spoke again. "You know what your muse is, don't you?"

He raised a brow and played dumb. "Who knows. It could be anything."

"Anything? Obviously, it was you hitting your head at the

hospital. It knocked some inspiration into you—literally," he chuckled, looking pleased at his own joke.

"Very funny." Aiden rubbed his forehead with the back of his hand. Thankfully, his scan had come out clear and there were no lasting effects from the fall, other than some bruising.

"I'm kidding. Of course it's a woman." Brandon smiled. "It's usually a woman."

Aiden shrugged casually. "Maybe, maybe not."

"Maybe not? Come on, Aiden. Both Colin and Darren said Abby looks just like Mandy. Seeing her must've triggered something in you. She brought you back to life."

"Have you been watching those Hallmark movies again? My life isn't nearly as dramatic. It wasn't like I was dying and she was the doctor who gave me CPR." Although the idea of her giving him mouth-to-mouth didn't seem like such a bad one. And here he was thinking about kissing a woman he barely knew. He shoved the crazy notion to the back of his mind, virtually locked it up, and threw away the key. "The reality is, we met because of a text I sent her by accident. We got set up on a blind date that went south. We met up again when she got into a car accident, and I had a panic attack, fainted, and knocked myself out. It sounds more like a satire if you ask me, not a romance."

"Oh, but you left out the part where you fell in love," Brandon snickered. "So, did you fall for her over text, at the restaurant, or in the hospital?"

Aiden scoffed. "Maybe you should start writing comedy since you think you're so funny."

"It's true though, isn't it? You like her. You wouldn't be avoiding the question if you didn't." He cocked his head as he mused, "This would make for a really interesting storyline, now that I think about it. You've got the plot twists, the conflict, and most of all, the angst. This could be a bestseller!"

"You are not writing about me, Brandon."

"Of course not. I'll change out the names and places," he joked.

Aiden shot him a glare. "What's gotten into you today? You are being way too funny for your own good and my good, too. Is there a girl to blame for this?"

"Hey, don't change the topic. We're talking about you."

Brandon sounded nonchalant, but the way his brother's cheeks reddened told Aiden he'd hit a nerve. So, there was a woman in the picture? "Is it Danica?"

"What? No way. Danica's a friend, a good friend, but nothing more. I'm working on setting her up with Darren."

"Oh yeah? You might want to make it clear to her then. I'm pretty sure she's interested in you."

"Why in the world would you think that?"

"From the way she talked about you when we were on our date. Abby also confirmed it. But you have to promise not to tell Danica that's how you know."

"You're trying to protect Abby now? I knew it. You do like her. So, when are you going to ask her out again?"

Aiden wiped his mouth and stuffed the napkin and his pair of chopsticks inside the now-empty take-out container. He set it on the table and leaned back in his chair. "I'm not."

"Why not?"

"She obviously doesn't want anything to do with me. She ran from the hospital room like she was escaping the plague. I'm not going to ask her out so she can reject me again." He could only take so much heartbreak. Not that he was truly heartbroken over Abby, but she reminded him so much of Mandy, he couldn't help feeling invested in their relationship, as non-existent as it was. "If she was interested, she wouldn't have left. She didn't even care if I had a head injury or not."

"She did ask how you're doing."

"What? When?"

"Colin said Candy got Abby's number before she left the

hospital. They've been texting each other ever since. She asked how your scan went."

Aiden wasn't sure which idea he was more curious about, his brother and his old girlfriend's sister being an item, or Abby showing concern for him. On second thought, it was definitely the latter. "Oh yeah?"

"Oh yeah," Brandon repeated with much more conviction. "You should give her a call, see how she's doing after her accident."

"I ... I don't know."

"Or at least text her."

He quirked a brow. "That's how this whole mess began, remember?"

"But it would make for an even cooler climax to the story than the one I was thinking of writing." He dug his phone out of his jacket pocket and began typing. "I need to take some notes so I don't forget."

"You're serious about making this into a book?"

"As serious as I am about seeing you happy. If you don't want to write your own happy ending, I will." He muttered to himself as he typed. "Reconcile with text message ..."

Ring!

Aiden traded curious looks with Brandon before reaching for his phone which sat on the far end of the table. The screen lit up and the sender's name—*Deejay*—immediately caught his eye. No way. "It can't be."

"What? Who is it?"

He held his phone up. Did Brandon or Candy put Abby up to this? "Was this your idea?"

Brandon's jaw dropped. "It wasn't me, bro, I promise. I couldn't have planned it better if I'd tried." He quickly dropped his gaze and began typing furiously. "This is fantastic."

Fantastic, it was not. If anything, it was freaky. What was he supposed to do now?

"Aiden, answer it before she hangs up!"

He gestured toward the hall to indicate he'd take the call in private. When he reached his bedroom, he closed the door. Swallowing hard, he swiped the screen to the left and answered, not knowing what to expect. Any hesitations he'd had about taking the call disappeared though as soon as he heard Abby's lovely voice.

Chapter Eighteen

ABBY

"Abby," he greeted her in an upbeat tone. "What a pleasant surprise."

Abby needed to get a grip. Aiden's voice had started a flurry of butterflies in her stomach as soon as he'd answered the phone. She fell back onto her bed and stared at the ceiling. Her posture reminded her too much of her younger self, the teenager who stared longingly at Aiden Spark's poster on her bedroom wall. She pushed away those memories and sat up. She was an adult now with a job to do. "Do you have a minute to talk? It won't take long."

"Of course." Aiden paused. "How are you?"

"I'm fine. You?"

"Good, thanks."

"Great," she began, trying to sound enthusiastic but professional. "So, I'm calling for business purposes. My cohost and I started a campaign on the air today called Play It Forward." She proceeded to fill him in on the details, starting with the phone calls they'd received that day and ending with Bria's nomination of him.

Aiden paused for a beat as if he were taking all the information in. "Wow, I'm surprised someone thought of me after all these years."

"I think more people would if they could find you online. I tried to tag you on social media, but you are nowhere to be found. That's why I had to call you."

He chuckled. "You make calling me sound like a bad thing. I hope it's not. I'm really happy you did."

Was he flirting or just being friendly? His tone made her wonder. "Well, texting you would've been worse. We both know how much trouble that's caused us." She decided to get to the point of her call. "Anyhow, can we count on you to play it forward?"

"Sure thing. I'd be honored to be involved. I bet you'll be able to make a huge impact with all these artists supporting you."

"Right?" His positive reaction boosted her confidence. Excitement flowed through her veins, making her chattier than she'd planned to be. "I feel the same way. We already had such a successful day. You wouldn't believe how excited people were. The calls kept coming in, and the stories people shared would melt even the Grinch's heart. It's amazing being a part of something so encouraging." She bit her lower lip, suddenly feeling shy. "Anyway, thank you for doing this."

"You're very welcome. Thank you for coming up with this idea."

"I'd like to take all the credit, but I have you to thank for it."

"Me? How so?"

"You know the verse about iron sharpening iron? You were like my iron, sharpening me and pushing me to do more. You were right, I do have a great platform. I'm going to use it for good from now on."

"I'm your personal iron? I like the sound of that."

Her whole body warmed at his words. She fanned herself with one hand and tried to play it cool. This was business, nothing more. He could say whatever sweet things he wanted to. She was not going to let him affect her. "Not mine specifically. A iron. An iron? You know what I mean."

He chuckled softly. "I do. I could say the same about you."

"What do you mean?" she asked cautiously.

"What you said to me at the hospital really made me think." He cleared his throat before he continued. "I know I've been hanging onto my grief for a long, long time. So long that I'd forgotten God's promises. You're the first person who helped me remember them. No one's bothered to challenge me about my faith, or lack of it, since Mandy died." He sighed. "Well, to be fair, I never shared everything I was going through with anyone, including my brothers. Growing up, they'd always looked up to me in whatever I did, academically, socially, spiritually. It didn't feel right to disappoint them, you know? I'm the oldest; I have a role to fulfill."

Abby blinked, not quite believing how raw and sincere Aiden sounded. Her heart ached for him, to know what he'd gone through, how lonely he must've been all these years. Even still, she felt the need to speak her mind. "You might be the oldest in the family, but it doesn't mean you have to be perfect. I hate to break it to you, but you're not perfect. Never have been, never will be. We're all human and flawed.

"There was a time when I tried to have it all together. I wanted to be the best sister I could be to my younger sister—to protect her and keep her from getting hurt. But there were too many variables out of my control. Our dad leaving was one of them. Then I fell for all the wrong guys and became this bitter person who was not fun to be around. I know all about being flawed." She sucked in a breath as she realized how much she'd revealed to Aiden. What was it about this guy that made her act like a bumbling fool? Perhaps it was better this way. Now he'd see her for who she was: everything that Mandy wasn't. "No one's perfect. That's why we need God. You don't have to deal with everything on your own. I don't think your brothers would want that for you. I imagine Mandy wouldn't have either."

"You're right. Thanks for reminding me." He blew out a long breath. "You know, it's nice to be able to talk to you. I feel like I can talk to you about anything. It's strange since we barely know each other."

"Yeah, well, maybe it's because we've struggled with some of the same things," she answered as nonchalantly as possible.

"Yeah, maybe. You know, I haven't felt this way since Mandy was alive. It almost feels like I'm talking to her——."

"Aiden, no." This was exactly what Abby was afraid of. "I'm not Mandy. I could never be. It sounds like she had some really big shoes to fill."

"No, she had the smallest feet. She wore a size six. She still fit into her favorite sneakers from seventh grade when she was in high school."

Abby looked down at her large feet encased in a pair of fuzzy slippers. They reflected how she felt: faded, worn out, and blue. If her life were a fairy tale, she'd play the role of Cinderella. If only there was a chivalrous man like the prince searching for her. It didn't matter though when her feet would never fit the dainty shoes of a princess. "Yeah, that wouldn't work. Mine are a size nine. I inherited these bad boys from my dad, along with my big mouth."

He chuckled softly. When he spoke again, his tone was nostalgic. "Mandy had the smallest mouth, too. She wore braces all throughout middle school, headgear and all. Thankfully, she only needed the headgear twelve hours a day. She hated it though, but I thought she looked cute. She made just about anything look cute ..." His voice trailed off.

Yep, he was still hung up on his old girlfriend. It was time to end the call and this—whatever it was. Abby squared her shoulders and set her jaw. "Hey, I need to go. It was nice chatting with you. Thanks for playing it forward. All of us at 103.1 appreciate—"

"Hold on," Aiden interrupted her. "Do you think we could have dinner again? I know our last date didn't end on the best terms. I'd like to try again if you're willing."

An image of his gorgeous smile popped into her head. Argh. Those dimples alone could make her lose her sense of reason. She longed to accept Aiden's invitation, but she wouldn't. Not when she knew he only wanted to spend time with her because she reminded him of the love of his life. "That's nice of you, but I don't think it's a good idea."

"If you're still upset about me leaving you with the bill, I promise I'll pay for that meal and this one, too. That's why you left the hospital, wasn't it? Because I was a jerk. I'm sorry I treated you direspect—"

"That's not why!" Abby had had enough of his apologizing. She'd heard stuff like this before from her ex and had believed him enough to take him back—time and time again. She'd bought into his lies, especially the one about her being too ugly for anyone else to love. Well, she was done with all of that. Even if no man loved her for who she was, God did. His love was enough. "Aiden, you need to face the facts. I can't be who you want me to be. You need to move on."

"I don't want to move on," he blurted. "I mean, I do want to move on from the past, but it's going to take time. But with your help, I think I can get there sooner, faster."

Was that all she was good for? "I can't be your crutch."

"Why? Is having a crutch a bad thing? Think of it as auto-tune. Even the best singers use it when their voice is shot. It's something they use when they need time to heal, to be their best."

Great. He was comparing her to a computer software? "I'm sorry to break it to you, but real artists don't use auto-tune. They suck it up and push through the hard times. You're going to have to find a way to get on with your life. I can't be a replacement for your old girlfriend. I can't be Mandy."

"Wh-what?" he spluttered. "Why would I want you to be Mandy?"

"Because I look like her. It's the only reason why you'd be interested in me."

"Is that what you think?"

"That's what I know." She lifted her glasses with the palm of her hand, feeling a trace of wetness on her cheek. She scolded herself for crying. Aiden Spark was not worth her tears. She wouldn't let him be. She tugged her robe around herself and whispered, "Take care, Aiden. Please don't call me again," she added before hanging up.

Chapter Nineteen

AIDEN

*A*iden slumped onto the carpet, his hand still clutching his phone. So much for trying to make things right with Abby. They'd been having a great conversation and getting along so well. She'd even divulged some personal information about her past to him. If that didn't show she trusted him, he didn't know what did. Why had she shut him out again?

His gaze landed on the photo sitting on his bedside table. He put his phone down and picked up the frame. He ran his finger over the glass, tracing the outline of her face. Was what Abby said true? Did he only enjoy her company because she reminded him of his first love? He had to admit that fact didn't hurt. But so much about Abby didn't resemble Mandy.

For starters, there was her voice. It was much louder and livelier, especially when their conversations got heated. There was also her temperament. Abby knew how to push his buttons like no one else did. She also spoke the truth to him when others wouldn't dare. Truth that made him reevaluate the way he'd been living and the lies he'd been believing. Such as the one about his past, that he'd never be able to move on from it.

But he no longer believed that. The trajectory of his life had changed when he met Abby, so much so that he felt at peace doing something he never thought he'd do. He kissed Mandy's photo, then tucked it away safely in a drawer. He was ready to start living—and loving—again.

A knock on the door paused his pondering. Aiden checked his watch and realized he'd been holed up in his room for a good twenty minutes. He called out for his brother to come in.

The door cracked open, letting in light from the hallway. Brandon stuck his head in and gave him a curious look. "Is everything okay? What happened with Abby?"

Aiden sighed. "The better question is, what didn't? She doesn't want anything to do with me, Bran. She told me to never call her again." He laughed wryly. "Which is a funny request, considering she's the one who keeps calling me."

His brother opened the door all the way and entered. "So, she called to tell you that?"

"No, she called about work." Aiden gave him a quick rundown of Abby's call. "So, is everything okay? Not really. But I can't do anything about it."

Brandon strode to the edge of the bed, taking slow but deliberate steps, like the question he posed next. "That's it?"

"What do you mean? Yes, that's it. She told me she thinks I'm only interested in her because she looks like Mandy. What am I supposed to say to that?"

"Well, is it true?"

"Of course not." He rose and began pacing, making a path from his bed to the door and back again. Running his hands through his hair, he tried to release his frustration. "I like who she is and how she's not afraid to speak her mind. She makes me think about things, things I haven't wanted to think about in a long, long time."

"About Mandy?"

He stopped and faced his brother. "No, about God."

Brandon's brows lifted. "Oh. I wasn't expecting that."

Pushing out a crooked smile, Aiden remarked, "To be honest, me neither."

"So, uh ..." Brandon stuck his hands in the pockets of his shorts and rocked on his heels. "Do you care to share ..."

"What I've been thinking about?"

"Yeah. Only if you want to," he added casually.

Aiden copied his brother's tone and answered, "Not really."

"You don't? Okay, it's cool—"

"I'm joking, Bran."

"Wow, and I thought we only had one actor in the family." He paused. "Wait, I take that back. You've been acting long before Evan ever did."

Even in the dim room, Aiden glimpsed sadness in his brother's eyes. "What are you talking about?"

"You've been putting on an act ever since Mandy died. Trying to be strong and in control, never asking for help from anyone. But the truth is you haven't been okay. Seeing you tonight, back to who you used to be, confirms it. This is who you're meant to be, the guy who cares about things like songwriting and eating good food and life and people."

He blinked twice, not believing the things coming out of Brandon's mouth. He'd never spoken so assertively before. But everything he said was true. "You're right. I haven't been myself. I lost my direction, I lost hope. I almost lost my faith. I've been mad at myself, but even more mad at God."

Brandon took a seat next to him. "It's okay to feel that way. He already knows how you feel. You can't hide it from him."

Aiden nodded. "I know. I'm working on talking to Him again. And trying to have faith, even about things that don't make sense. This thing with Abby is certainly one of them. I don't know what to do. How do I convince her I like her for who she is? Come on, you're the romance writer. What would your characters do to win over the girl?"

"Uh, do you want the creative answer or the canned one?"

"Both."

"Well, it's one and the same, really. It depends on how you want to do it."

"So, what is it?" He tapped his foot impatiently, his toes leaving imprints in the plushy carpet. "How do I convince Abby?"

Brandon grinned. "With a grand romantic gesture. You know the kind where the guy does something crazy and unexpected like serenading her in front of a crowd or—" his eyes lit up "—saving her life!"

"I think I'll leave the life-saving to Darren," Aiden answered. "But singing—I can do that. I can definitely do that." The gears in his head were giving off virtual sparks with how fast they were turning. He would use Abby's love of music to his advantage. Even if she wouldn't listen to him, she'd listen to her favorite band. "It's going to take a miracle to make it happen, but I'm going to try."

"What's going to take a miracle?"

Aiden grabbed his phone off the table. "Getting Heartland back together. I haven't talked to the guys in ages. I'm sure they still hate me." Without his presence as the lead singer, sales had dwindled to the point where the record label ended their contract. He had effectively ended all their careers when he left. "It's going to take an act of God to get them to agree to do this favor for me."

"Then we better ask for His divine intervention."

"Uh, okay, sure." Asking God for help wasn't the first thing that came to mind, especially since he'd ignored Him for so many years, but it was the right—and best—thing to do. "Like now?"

"Of course, right now."

"All right." Aiden closed his eyes and bowed his head. When almost ten seconds had passed in silence, he opened one eye to find his brother staring at him in amusement. "Are you going to pray?"

"I was waiting for you to."

"Me?" He felt a bit rusty and out of practice, but he'd been a

Christian long enough to know that words didn't matter. As long as he had faith—and he was beginning to get some of it back now—God would hear him. He nodded and shut his eyes. "God, I need Your help. You know how much I like Abby. Thank you for bringing her into my life. I'm sorry I messed up the first time around with her, but I'd like another chance. Please help me make it possible. Thank you. In Jesus's name, amen."

Brandon clapped him on the shoulder and smiled. "You're back, bro. What a relief. Now I don't have to play the part of the older, bossy brother anymore."

"Ha," Aiden smirked. "It's called leading, not bossing. That's what leaders do."

He rolled his eyes. "Whatever you call it, you do it well. I have a feeling you'll have the band back together in no time. What guy in their right mind would turn down the chance to have girls screaming their name?"

"Uh, these aren't teenagers we're talking about. Our fans are all grown up. They're women in their thirties now."

"Hey, there's nothing wrong with that age group. They're the ones who buy my books. Speaking of, I can put the word out for you on social media since you don't have an online presence. Or I could help get you started on that," Brandon added hopefully.

Aiden smiled. "Sure. I'll do it for Abby's sake." She was worth giving up his privacy for. He'd do just about anything to get her to talk to him again. God willing, she would.

Chapter Twenty

ABBY

*A*bby peered out the passenger window of Candy's car. She spotted her old sedan parked in the mechanic's lot. Or what she thought was her car. The vehicle appeared to have gone through a makeover. It now boasted a new coat of shiny red paint, and a crack on the front windshield had been fixed. She squinted at the license plate, noting the familiar numbers and letters. Yup. It was her car, all right.

"I take it from the way your mouth's hanging open that you approve," Candy piped up next to her in the driver's seat. "Your car almost looks like new."

Swallowing her shock, Abby nodded. Almost two months had passed since the car accident, and if anyone had told her then how much she'd appreciate getting her car wrecked, she would've thought they were crazy. But hindsight was twenty-twenty. In the weeks since, she'd made a new friend. Candy was like the older sister she never had. A bit headstrong, but with good intentions. And one of them was ensuring Abby didn't need to take public transportation anymore. "I love it. But I can't afford this extra stuff. I had to borrow money from you just to fix it."

"Hey, don't worry about it." Candy waved her hand to end her protests. She parked her car and turned to face Abby. "Consider this an early Christmas present from me. If you like it, I'm happy. Receive the blessing."

Abby opened her mouth again to protest, but held back. Instead, she chewed on her lower lip as she stared out the window again. What a blessing indeed, and yet another reminder of God's grace in her life. Who was she to turn it down? She met Candy's gaze. "Okay, I receive it. But I'm still going to pay you back for the repairs."

Candy tapped her French-manicured nails on the steering wheel and pursed her red lips. "About that ..."

"What?" Quirking a brow, Abby balked. "I can't let you pay for that, too. It cost a few thousand dollars!"

"Oh, I'm not paying for it. Someone else offered to."

The playful lilt of her voice, along with the wide-eyed, innocent look she gave her, told Abby more than she wanted to know. "You can't possibly be talking about Aiden."

"Of course I am. And why wouldn't I be? He's the only thing the tabloids talk about these days," she joked. "Or haven't you noticed?"

Oh, she'd noticed. Aiden Sparks had done a complete about-face and given up his privacy, totally and completely. It all started when one of his students—who was also a listener of the station—sent in a photo of him. Not a photo taken in secret, but a selfie taken by the professor himself, with his class in the background.

Soon after, Marcus informed her Aiden was now on social media—everywhere. News about him spread quickly after that as the paparazzi started showing up at the college and his home. She saw the headlines and photos whenever she stood in line at the grocery store. Or opened up the celebrity news sites. Headlines such as, *Former Heartland Hottie Back in the Spotlight* and *Meet America's Hottest Professor!* There were also the obviously fake ones: *Aiden Sparks Reunites with Old Flame* and *Aiden Sparks Spotted with New Love*. Abby only knew the latter were false because Candy gave her lengthy updates on Aiden whenever possible. He was keeping his distance like she'd told him to.

"He doesn't need to do anything for me," Abby insisted. "It's my problem to deal with."

"He's not doing this out of obligation, Abby. Don't you get it? He cares about you." Candy took a deep breath and released it. "You're the first thing he's cared about since—"

"Let me guess. Since Mandy?" She didn't mean to be rude and interrupt, but she'd heard enough about Aiden's incredible girl-friend. Enough to know she'd never live up to her.

"Yes." Candy tilted her head and studied her. "I hope you know how big of a deal this is. When Mandy died, a big part of Aiden died, too. He went through a really rough patch. He did plenty of things he regrets to this day. He didn't tell me these things, but he didn't have to. You could see it in the way he lived. He lost his passion for music. He lost hope and faith in anything good coming his way. For you to come along and change all that is nothing short of a miracle. Colin, his other brothers, and I—we're all incredibly grateful. But the most grateful person of all is Aiden. Him doing things for you is his way of showing you that. That's all."

That's all? Didn't he realize how much this one act was chipping away at the armor around her heart? "I appreciate it, but it's too much. He should've sent me a card."

"Not when you told him never to contact you again. Anyhow, a card isn't enough when a man's trying to make things right with the woman he likes."

Abby swallowed hard. The idea that Aiden would be interested in her had her all flustered. She adjusted her glasses with her palm, wishing she could hide her now-flaming face behind her hands. When she trusted herself to speak, she retorted, "It doesn't matter though because I'm not interested in him."

"Then why do you hang onto my every word when I talk about him?"

"I ..."

"I rest my case."

The way Candy narrowed her eyes almost made Abby squirm in her seat. This wasn't someone to mess with, even for her. "There's a problem though."

"What? Tell me what it is and I'll make it go away."

Abby had to laugh. Was this how an older sibling spoke to a younger one? Apparently so. "Thanks for offering, but even you can't do anything about this. The only reason Aiden wants my attention is because of who I remind him of."

Candy chuckled, softly at first, then loudly. "Is that what you think? Because you are *nothing* like my sister."

"Believe me, I know. I've heard what an amazing person she was. But it doesn't do away with the fact that I look like her."

"Oh, you may look alike, but when you open your mouth, all bets are off. My sister was the sweetest, most soft-spoken person there was. If you needed a real-life example of meekness, she was it. You, on the other hand—" she pointed at herself "—you're like me. When God handed out the loud, opinionated genes, he gave both of us an extra dose. There's nothing wrong with that. We're just wired differently. Which is how I know that when Aiden sees you—most definitely, when he hears you—he hears Abby. And he likes you for who you are. He really does."

She didn't know whether to be offended or happy. Okay, she was happy, according to the flutters in her stomach. Was Candy right? Did Aiden like her for her? "Even if what you're saying is true, the thing is, we hardly know each other. What if he gets to know me—all my baggage and hang-ups—and decides it's too much? I-I've been rejected before; I don't want to go through that again." She crossed her arms over her chest. "It's not worth it. No guy is worth getting your heart trampled on. Not even America's hottest professor," she added with a smirk.

"Hey." Candy placed a hand on Abby's arm. "I'm sorry you got hurt before. But Aiden is as faithful as they come. He stood by my sister through her darkest days. He won't abandon you when things get tough. If anything, I'm more worried about him and what would happen if you ended up breaking his heart—so, don't do that, you hear?"

Ha! She, break Aiden Spark's heart? That would be the day. Abby wanted to say something sarcastic in response, but the glint in Candy's eyes stopped her. The woman was serious. Abby held up both hands in surrender. "I hear you loud and clear."

"Great." A pleased smile softened Candy's features. "You won't refuse then when I tell you Aiden needs you to emcee a concert he's putting together."

"Say what? A concert? When and where?"

"November tenth at The Masonic in S.F."

Abby's jaw dropped. "In five days? Why haven't I heard anything about this?"

"It all came together this past week. Aiden's planning to make an announcement on social media tomorrow. He's certain the tickets will sell out. All the recent publicity he's been getting should help."

"For sure. But why the sudden interest in putting together a concert? And with returning to the spotlight? I thought he wanted to put all that celebrity stuff behind him. This makes no sense."

"Abby, this is his way of playing it forward like you asked him to. The concert is for charity to raise money for pediatric cancer research. He knew for it to be successful, he had to attach—"

"His name to it," Abby finished for her. Hot tears pricked her eyes as all the pieces of the equation fell into place. She was beginning to understand Aiden's intentions and how grand they were. And selfless. He was willing to give up his life of privacy and use his celebrity status for good. Like she had suggested when she'd accused him of being uncaring. He had listened to her big mouth and followed through.

Tears began to cascade down her face. She swiped at them,

trying to prevent a full-on blubbering session. Oh, she was such a softie! She couldn't help it though. The thought of a man—an influential, smart, and hot man!—doing something so sweet and amazing turned her insides into mush.

"I can't ... believe ... he did ... all this," she managed to get out in between her sobs.

"Believe it. He's like a new person because of you. Well, mostly because of you. I'd like to take some of the credit, too, for all the times I prayed for him over the years."

Abby shook her head. "The real credit goes to God."

Candy smiled. "I know; I was kidding."

She took a shaky breath, not knowing whether to laugh or cry. "I'm such a mess. I'm happy, really I am. I'm just blown away by all of this."

"I'm happy, too, and relieved. I can finally stop worrying about Aiden. I know he'll be in good hands with you."

Those kind words started her bawling again. She took the tissue Candy handed her and blew her nose. The loud, honking sound that came out made them both laugh. "Are you sure about that?"

"Yes, I'm sure."

Abby nodded. For the first time in a long time, she felt certain, too. Certain there were too many coincidences for her to not believe God's hand was in this. And certain Aiden was worth taking a chance on. Now if there was some way for her to tell him that.

Chapter Twenty-One

AIDEN

*A*iden took a deep breath as he walked into the brightly-lit dressing room of The Masonic. Memories flooded his mind of himself standing in this very place years ago as he and his bandmates waited to go on stage. Today, however, he was alone, at least for the time being.

He'd arrived extra early to make sure everything was in place for the evening's concert. A concert that was nothing short of miraculous, considering how quickly he'd put it together. He'd expected to wait until the new year to secure a venue, but somehow by God's grace, he'd managed to book this one when another artist canceled two days ago. Moreover, the tickets had sold out within three hours, all thanks to fans tweeting and retweeting about it. He had to admit, he had some of the best fans around, loyal ones who liked and followed him on social media the very day he set up his accounts. The support they gave him was overwhelming and humbling at the same time. Even still, there was one person he longed to hear from who had yet to contact him.

He'd given up his private life in hopes of hearing from Abby. He now had paparazzi showing up at the college and trying to sneak into his lectures. Thankfully, the administrators didn't mind the attention; they considered it as free advertising for the school. His students were also understanding and even proud of his new ridiculous title as "America's hottest professor". Several asked to take pictures with him for their older relatives and also brought in old Heartland CDs for him to sign. He was sure the novelty would wear off in time, but for the moment, he was enjoying his celebrity status. Most of all, he was using it for good, as Abby had asked him to.

Abby. He'd been praying about her, and for her, non-stop. For a guy who hadn't talked to God in years, the words flowed like water when he thought of her. He wanted the Lord's blessing to pursue her, but more so, to not mess things up more than he had already. The fact she had agreed to emcee the concert was a good sign. The still doubtful part of him wanted to confirm with Candy that Abby was indeed coming.

He dug his phone out of his back pocket and took a seat on one of the plush sofas. In the years since he'd performed here, The Masonic had gone through some major renovations. The dressing room now looked like a luxury hotel suite, complete with floor-to-ceiling mirrors and a full bar.

Ding, ding!

His phone vibrated with an incoming text. He swiped the screen open and read the message, his heart sinking in the process. No, why today? Before he could reply to the text, the phone rang.

He hoped it wasn't more bad news. "Hello?"

"Hey Aiden," Nick, the oldest one of his bandmates answered him groggily. "I don't think I'm going to make it tonight. I'm so sorry, man, but I literally can't get out of my hotel bed."

"What happened? Are you all right?"

"I'm fine, but feeling my age. I was practicing that one move where we get down on the ground and jump back up, you know? I did something to my lower back, pulled a muscle. The doctor gave me something for the pain and ordered me to stay put."

Aiden didn't know whether to laugh or cry. "I'm sorry to hear that. I guess we overdid it this week trying to relearn those dance moves."

"I'm nearing forty, man. These hips don't move like they used to. Anyhow, you'll have to do the show without me."

"I don't think we can do the show at all now." He rose and began pacing the room. "Kevin can't make it either. He texted me saying his wife's in labor. He needs to catch the next flight home."

"You're kidding. How about Brian? Half the band is better than none."

"I don't know—"

Ding!

An incoming text cut him off. As he suspected, it was from Brian. *I can't make it. Accidentally had a milkshake at lunch. Stuck in the bathroom. Sorry.*

How did one drink a milkshake by accident? "I was right. Brian texted to say he's not coming either. Something to do with lactose intolerance."

Nick scoffed. "More like stage fright. He always hated performing."

"Either way, there's only me left." He shook his head in disbelief. "This is not how I imagined today going." Aiden was starting to think it wasn't meant to be. Had he gone to all this trouble for nothing? How was he supposed to put on a Heartland concert without the headlining act? If people demanded a refund, he wouldn't have anything to give to charity. "What am I going to do?"

"Do what you do best, Aiden. Put on a show."

"By myself?"

"Yeah, why not? The fans liked your solos the most. So, give them what they want: a night with Aiden Spark. Sing our old songs and do some covers. Do you have any new material?"

"One song, but it's an important one."

"Great, you're set then. All you need to do is sing your heart out."

He'd be doing that in more ways than one. If all went well, by the end of the night, Abby would know how he felt about her. And maybe, just maybe, he'd find out how she felt.

He promptly ended the call with Nick. First, he needed to find the stage manager and inform her of the changes. He also needed to do a sound check and get in the right mindset for the show. He was already out of practice, and he hadn't planned on doing a whole concert by himself. Fortunately, he had grown a full set of calluses and could play his guitar without any pain. He hoped his voice would hold up as well.

On second thought, he decided to sit down for a moment to pray. With only an hour until the show started, he needed all the help he could get. He bowed his head and closed his eyes.

Lord, You've provided so many miracles, from bringing me back to you, to putting this concert together, to helping me meet Abby. But things are starting to fall apart. And part of me wonders if I did something wrong for this to happen ... but the other part believes You have everything under control. So, I'm choosing to have faith. I trust You. Thanks for helping me, for loving me.

Aiden opened his eyes and took a deep breath. A great sense of peace flooded his body, the kind that surpassed human understanding. Under the circumstances, he should be stressed, or at the very least frustrated, but he knew he'd done his best. He was leaving the rest in God's hands.

He wiped away the tears that had gathered in his eyes and smiled. This was the start of a new chapter in his life. And what better way to begin than to do what he loved the most.

With a new purpose to his steps, he made his way to the door and opened it. As he strode down the hallway, he began humming scales to warm up his vocal cords. A potential song list ran through his mind and he pulled his phone from his pocket to jot some notes down. With both thumbs flying across the screen, he rounded the corner and promptly collided with someone headed his way.

"Ow!"

Aiden reached out to catch the woman he had crashed into. "Sorry, I didn't see you!"

"It's okay. I didn't see you either," she mumbled into his chest. She looked up and gasped when their eyes met. "Aiden."

His body warmed at the sight of this beautiful woman he couldn't get off his mind. Her face was now inches away from his, as were the full, pink lips that had uttered his name. "Abby. You came."

"Of course—oh!" Her cheeks flushed when she realized her hands were still on his chest. She smiled sheepishly and quickly dropped them to her side. "Of course, I came. I wouldn't have missed this concert ... or the chance to see you again," she added with a coy smile. "This is a wonderful thing you're doing."

Relief flooded his whole being when he heard her words. "It's all because of you, Abby. You gave me the push I needed to do something more with my life. I can't thank you enough."

"No, *I'm* the one who should be thanking you. You paid for my car repairs, even after I hung up on you. That was so not cool of me—"

Aiden cut her off with a shake of his head. "Don't worry about it. I did a lot worse. Don't forget I walked out on our date and left you to pay the bill. If anyone should be apologizing, it's me."

Abby pursed her lips for a moment. "You've got a point there," she replied with a glint in her eye.

He laughed. "I'm glad we finally agree on something."

"Well, apology accepted, if you'll accept mine." She held out her hand. "Deal?"

"Of course," he agreed wholeheartedly. "Deal."

When their fingers touched, Aiden felt a weight lift from his shoulders. The handshake may have been a playful gesture, but it was a gesture of reconciliation nonetheless. With it came the reassurance that God had heard his prayers and answered them. Abby was here, and she looked even more beautiful than he remembered. Her simple black dress hugged her curves and showed off her legs. A red headband held back her thick hair and complemented her fair complexion. What he adored most, however, was her confidence. The way she met his gaze head-on, unblinking, almost teasing him. He didn't mind being held captive by those big brown eyes.

The air sparked with an unseen electricity, emboldening Aiden. He clasped her palm and turned it over to rest on top of his. In one swift motion, he lifted her hand to his lips and kissed it.

Abby's eyes widened. "What was that for?"

"I thought I'd sweeten the deal."

"Are you trying to one-up me?" Her grin reflected the humor in her voice. "You should know I'm a very worthy opponent."

"Not anymore. I want to be fighting the good fight with you now, not against you."

"What are you saying, Aiden?"

He longed to speak more from his heart, but lost the chance to when a man called out from down the hall, "Mr. Spark! It's time for your sound check."

Aiden reluctantly turned and acknowledged the stagehand with a wave. He offered Abby a pained smile. "I'm sorry, I have to go."

She squeezed his hand before letting go. "Don't be. The show can't start without its star. Go on. Break a leg."

As much as Aiden loved performing, he wished he could pause time. There were so many things he wanted to say to Abby, but they would have to wait. Not for much longer though. "We'll finish this conversation soon," he reassured her before he walked away.

EPILOGUE

Encore

*A*bby waited on the side of the stage for her cue to enter. Her chest swelled with pride as she thought of the work Aiden had put in to make this concert successful. From her vantage point, she glimpsed dozens of people—mostly women her age—standing in the general admission area. Beyond them sat hundreds more concert goers, both on the floor and in the balcony sections. The venue had been renovated to fit over three thousand attendees, and it looked to be a packed house tonight. The buzz of excitement in the air added to the adrenaline running through her veins. She enjoyed every opportunity when music brought people together. This night was no exception.

A stagehand approached and handed her a mic. He motioned for her to take the stage. She took a deep breath and said a quick prayer of thanks to God. So many emotions ran through her body, causing her hands to tremble, but strangely enough, she felt at peace. Peace in knowing God loved her and she was where He meant for her to be. Everything else was minor details that would eventually fall into place. Including Aiden Spark who—she was happy to admit—had moved to the top of that list.

Their intimate moment may have been cut short earlier, but

Abby had faith they would talk again. She also had hope, hope that a relationship with Aiden could—and would—be different from her others. He was a different man than her exes; she was in a different place than she had been in the past. Most importantly, they both had a relationship with the Lord. He had brought them this far and would continue to sustain them.

She clung to this truth as she walked onto the stage and toward whatever the future held.

Blinking against the bright lights, she smiled and waved to the crowd. "How's everyone doing?"

Applause immediately resonated in the circular-shaped building.

"Hi, I'm Abby from 103.1, the number one station in the Bay Area station for today's hits. Have we got a show for you tonight! We're going old school and taking it back a decade to bring you America's favorite boy band. Let's give it up for Heartland!" She clapped and walked off stage as the curtain rose.

Women began shrieking, their voices joined together to create a high-pitched frenzy. Abby would've screamed, too, if she weren't on duty. The thought of her favorite boy band taking the stage at this very moment gave her chills. She looked back, expecting to see four men, but only Aiden stood there, a guitar in his hands.

He stepped up to the mic and greeted everyone, as if he did this sort of thing every night. He was a natural on stage with his confident stance and the charming smile Abby recognized from his younger days.

Aiden was a star, always had been and always would be. It was evident when he opened his mouth to sing. Upon hearing the first few notes, she might've swooned a little. Okay, she swooned a lot, especially when he glanced her way for a split second. Their eyes met, and she had to remind herself to breathe. Her body warmed remembering how it felt to be near him, to touch him. No man ever looked at her the way he had— as if he really saw her. Not only that; he liked what he saw. What a wonderful—yet crazy—thing it was to be on the receiving end of such affection. It was yet another reminder of God's grace to her.

After Aiden sang his first song—a Heartland classic—he began speaking. All eyes were focused on center stage where he stood in the spotlight. She admired the ease with which he spoke to the audience.

"You may have noticed it's only me here tonight. Due to unforeseen circumstances, the rest of the band couldn't make it. God wasn't surprised by any of this though, and I believe He has everything under control. I hope you'll stick around and enjoy the rest of this night with me. I've got a full set to sing for you, both old and new songs, that I think you'll enjoy."

Several women in the audience called out, "We love you, Aiden!"

He grinned in response and began strumming a few chords. Abby immediately recognized another one of Heartland's hits and began clapping. Memories of herself singing along to this song as a high schooler came to mind. Who knew she'd one day be standing twenty feet from her crush and listening to him sing live? Her inner teenager wanted to squeal. Once a Heartland fan, always a Heartland fan. This fact rang truer now that she knew the man behind the song. He who was so much more than a pop star. He was kind, giving, and strong, and someone she was falling for more and more.

Aiden finished singing and suddenly turned in her direction. He gestured for her to join him. "Abby, please join me."

What?! Why was he calling her over? She shook her head adamantly. There was a reason she worked in radio. She didn't mind deejaying or briefly emceeing a concert, but there was no way she was going to be the center of attention.

Aiden didn't seem to understand this, because the next thing she knew, he was walking over to her. He reached her side and held out his hand. He mouthed the word *please* and gave her the most endearing smile. Before she could think clearly, she had placed her hand in his.

He pulled her on stage and introduced her to the crowd. "You probably recognize this woman from her job on the radio, but she is more than a pretty voice or face. Abby Dearan is very special to me. She came into my life—actually, God brought her into my life —when I needed her the most."

Abby squeezed out a shaky smile as she stared wide-eyed at Aiden. What was he doing?

"Not only is she beautiful on the outside, she has a beautiful heart. Because of her persuasion, I decided to put on this concert to raise money for cancer research." He took a deep breath. "Several years ago, I lost someone I loved to cancer. Afterwards, I lost my desire to sing, too. But thanks to Abby, I picked up my guitar again. I also started writing. I'd like to sing my newest song that I wrote for you."

Abby's chest tightened when she realized Aiden was speaking to her. "Me? You wrote a song for me?"

He leaned in to whisper in her ear. "It's one of the perks of dating a pop star, in case you were open to the idea. I meant what I said about being on the same side."

His masculine scent, paired with his warm breath tickling her ear, made her mind go blank. She nodded and let her dopey grin do the talking.

Aiden released her hand and picked up his guitar. As he plucked a melody on the strings, he began singing.

Abby stood rooted in place, her heart softening with each note. A trail of tears reached her chin before she realized she was crying. She'd never heard such a beautiful song before, and to think it was written for her.

When the song ended, Aiden stepped away from the mic. He set down his guitar, then reached for her hand. He laced his fingers between hers and gave them a gentle squeeze. Even with thousands of people watching, he only had eyes for her. "Thanks for trusting me enough to join me on stage. I meant every word I said. I believe God brought you into my life. He had mercy on me for some reason."

"Because He loves you," she answered him simply. "He doesn't give up on the people He loves. And boy, He must love me a whole lot, too, because I don't deserve any of this. The song, you singing to me—my teenage self is freaking out right now. My adult self is freaking out, too."

One side of his mouth curved up in a tender smile. "I'm feeling like a teenager, too, and it's not because of these boy band songs I'm singing. You make me feel young again, Abby." He touched her face, running his calloused thumb ever-so-gently down her cheek. "It's taking everything in me to not kiss you right now."

A thrill shot through her body at the thought of his mouth on hers. "Why don't you?"

"It'd be nice not to share our first kiss with three thousand people watching."

"Good point." She narrowed her eyes as an idea came to her. "Hold that thought."

She walked over to the mic stand and addressed the sea of eager faces. "Thanks for your patience, everyone. We've got more music and more of Aiden Spark for you coming up. Right now, we're going to break for intermission. Go stretch your legs, grab some food, and come back in fifteen."

A curtain fell upon the stage, enveloping them in their own world. Abby turned to find Aiden at her side with a knowing smile on his face.

"Using your powers as emcee to your advantage?"

She laughed. "It's one of the perks of dating a deejay, in case you were open to the idea."

"Oh, I'm definitely open to it." Aiden pulled her into his arms and rested his forehead against hers. He gently nudged the tip of her nose with his. "How about you? How do you feel about dating an old pop star?"

"A pop star who's also America's Hottest Professor? I'm definitely signing up for his class. And don't worry, I won't miss any of my office hour appointments," she joked.

"I'll send you a text if you ever do," he winked.

She rolled her eyes. "No more texts. Let's stick to talking on the phone or face-to-face."

"Agreed." He paused with a smile. "What about mouth-to-mouth?"

"Mouth-to-mouth? Like CPR?"

"No, like this." He tipped her chin up and leaned in.

"Oh!" She gasped as his mouth claimed hers. Warmth zinged through her entire body from her cheeks to her toes. The kiss deepened, and Abby had to grab onto Aiden's arms to keep from melting to the floor. She should've known he'd kiss as well as he sang! When they pulled apart, she took a quick breath and leaned in again to bridge the gap between them. As much as she enjoyed talking, she could get used to this kind of non-verbal communication.

"Hey, we're really going to need CPR if we keep this up," Aiden murmured in between several more kisses.

Abby pulled back, squinting as she looked up at him through her now-fogged up lenses. She raised her glasses with the palm of her hand to see more clearly. "This has never happened before."

"You do know you're kissing America's *hottest* professor?"

She groaned. "And the corniest one, too, apparently."

"Are you having second thoughts now?"

The uncertainty in his voice tugged at her heart. Second thoughts? No. Freaking. Way. Abby shook her head, his gorgeous face now in clear view. "You've got me, Aiden. All of me—the good, the bad, and the ugly. If anyone should be having second thoughts, it's you."

He narrowed his eyes, holding her gaze steady and sure. "I see you, Abby, and what I see is nowhere near ugly. You are absolutely, one hundred percent—"

"Beautiful?" she finished for him in a playful tone.

"Exactly. You read my mind."

"It's not hard to," she teased him, "when you say the same line over and over."

"I only say it because it's true."

"You might want to think about switching it up now and then. You know, throw in some other adjectives like brilliant, funny or incredible. I wouldn't mind hearing those things."

"All right. Abby, you are brilliant, funny, incredible, and amazingly beautiful," he added with a grin. "And I'll keep on telling you these things until you believe them yourself."

Without a doubt, his words had already started to sink in. "It's working. But you can still say them even after I believe them. There's no need to stop with the compliments, you know."

"You got it." Chuckling, Aiden wrapped his arms around her more tightly. "There's no need to stop with the kissing either."

"I'm afraid there is. You have a show to do," she reminded him. "How about we kiss more later?"

"Deal."

Abby cupped his face and planted a loud smack on his lips. "All right, America's Hottest Professor, go do what you do best. Sing!"

―――――

Be sure to check out Brandon and Bria's story, *A Sudden Spark*, book two in The Spark Brothers series.

He's a writer too shy to speak to women. She's a single mom who's sworn off men. Little do they know how much a marriage of convenience will shake up their lives.

Brandon Spark may know a thing or two about women as a romance author, but his real love life proves otherwise. Between his hang-up over a college friend and bouts with social anxiety, dating is the last thing on his mind ... until he runs into his old crush.

Hair stylist Bria Montgomery made some major mistakes a decade ago—wandering from her faith, then getting pregnant and dropping out of college. She's desperate to leave her past—and the men from it—behind, but it's impossible when they keep showing up in her life.

Brandon can't believe he has a second chance with his first love; Bria can't fathom ever falling for a guy she friend-zoned years ago. When an unexpected custody battle forces them to become husband and wife, things get intense and personal—fast.

Will this sudden change end their friendship or spark a lasting romance?

———

Check out Chapter One of *A Sudden Spark* here ...

Brandon Spark ran his arm across his forehead, catching the beads of moisture gathered there. He groaned. The bookstore had turned up the air conditioning to compensate for the mid-June heat wave, yet he was still sweating. He closed his eyes and tried visualizing his happy place, the quiet sanctuary of his study where he worked. Outside the window, birds sang a cheerful tune; inside, a candle burned with his favorite citrus scent. He placed himself in the picture and felt the tension in his shoulders melt away ... until some high-pitched screams penetrated his bubble.

Yikes. His eyes popped open. This could mean only one thing. His fans were already arriving for today's meet and greet. It was a good thing he'd set multiple alarms to make sure he'd gotten here early. The author event wasn't set to start for another twenty minutes, but there they were, fast approaching the corner of the store where he sat behind a small table. His heart began racing again at the thought of socializing for the next hour.

How he longed for solitude. His fingers itched to get back to his laptop. Just hours earlier, he had been downing his third cup of coffee while he worked on his latest novel. He was right on schedule to finish the story, if he could only find a way to end it. He needed something better than *And they lived happily ever after*. His readers wouldn't be happy with a generic ending like that.

After successfully publishing ten romance books within the last two years, one would think he'd have this genre down. Actually, he did. He could plot out character profiles, story arcs, and conflict resolution in his sleep. His imagination had always been his strong suit ever since he was a kid. Whereas his four brothers excelled in talent, humor, strength, and charm, he majored in dreams—daydreams to be exact.

He'd been the kid who lived at the library while his brothers played outside. As they grew up, he became the teenager who made up his own stories and scribbled them down in his journals instead of going out on dates. Now, at age thirty-one, he created stories in the comfort of his two-bedroom condo in a suburb outside of San Francisco. Not much had changed, except that he now made money selling books to eager women looking for happily-ever-afters.

Which was why he needed this book to end the way his readers liked—in a swoon-worthy yet believable way.

Brandon leaned back in his chair and released a heavy breath. He hated reading stories that didn't have a happy ending. But he also hated romance that made love seem easy and cheap. He'd grown up in a Christian home and knew all the Bible verses about love by heart. The passage from First Corinthians chapter thirteen that listed the attributes of love was one of his favorites. He'd witnessed his parents' marriage— thirty-five years next month—and how earnest and committed they were to each other. That's the kind of love he hoped to portray in his books.

His one problem though? He'd never experienced a relationship like that. Or any serious one for that matter.

A young blonde woman appeared at Brandon's side. "Don't worry, Bran. You're going to do great. I'm praying for you."

"Thanks, Danica." He squeezed out a grateful smile in response to the store owner's sympathetic one. He took several deep breaths, hoping to tame the anxiety gnawing at his chest. "I really appreciate you having me here again. As hard as these in-person events are, I know they're good for me and my sales."

"They're good for the store, too. I ordered an extra box of your books for today since we sold out last time." She gave his arm a friendly squeeze. "I brought some extra make-up wipes, too, in case the ladies get a little overzealous with the kissing."

He winced, remembering the lipstick stains Danica had insisted on wiping off for him at his last book signing. He'd appreciated her effort, but the gesture had been too close for comfort. He didn't want her getting the wrong idea about their friendship. That's why he had come prepared this time. He took out a small pack of wipes from his pocket. "Thanks, but I can clean myself up today. You'll likely have your hands full with all the purchases."

A hurt look crossed Danica's face, but she quickly composed herself and nodded. "Yeah, that's a good idea." She backed up and gestured to the small crowd gathering before them. "I'll tell everyone to have a seat. We'll start when you're ready."

Brandon nodded gratefully then wiped at the sweat on his brow again.

Buzz!

His cell phone sitting on the table vibrated with an incoming call. *Number One* flashed across the screen. A sense of relief fell on him to see the familiar words. "Aiden, thanks for calling."

"Hey, bro, of course." The smooth voice of one of America's hottest boy band members came over the line. His older brother, Aiden, had held that title as a teenager, but recent events in his life—specifically a woman—had brought him back into the limelight. "Are you at the bookstore already?"

"I'm here, trying my best not to faint, although that sounds like a good option right about now."

Aiden scoffed. "Don't worry, you're going to do great. Isn't this your third signing? You're a pro by now."

"It's my fourth, and I'm nowhere near being a pro. I do everything my therapist told me to do—take omega 3s, deep breathing, visualizing—but my body still goes into fight-or-flight mode." Brandon rubbed his chest to ease the tension building there. "I wish I could handle public speaking like you do. You thrive on stage; I barely make it out alive."

"Hey, you're not helping yourself by thinking like that. Getting stuck in negative thoughts only pulls you down further. Have you prayed about this? Unloaded your worries to the Lord? That helps me with my nerves before a performance."

One corner of Brandon's mouth curved up. It was both surprising and comforting to hear Aiden talk like this. After a decade of trying to help his brother renew his faith in God, the tables had switched. Now Aiden was the one encouraging him. "I haven't yet, but thanks for the reminder."

"Just returning the favor," he quipped with a smile in his voice. "Is this signing at Danica's bookstore again?"

"Yeah, it is. She's really good about supporting indie authors. I got quite a few new readers from the last one I did here."

"Are you sure she's not just good at supporting one author in particular?"

Brandon raised a brow. His brother had been making a lot of implications about Danica lately. He guessed Aiden's girlfriend, Abby, was encouraging him in the background since she and Danica were best friends. He lowered his voice as he reiterated, "Like I told you before, there's nothing going on between us."

"You're not interested in her at all? She's a great girl, a solid believer, and you both love to read."

"I know she's great. I just don't see her that way. She doesn't make me feel the way Abby makes you feel, you know?" Brandon paused, trying to grasp the right words. "Like time stops when the two of you are together and nothing else matters."

Silence ensued, followed by a soft chuckle. "A year ago, I would've said you're a hopeless romantic, but I actually understand what you mean now. You're right, you can't force yourself to feel something for a person, no matter how great they are or how much they may like you."

"You can't. Believe me, I've thought about it. I was flattered she would even consider me. But I think she'd be happier with someone like Darren. She's always talking about the alpha heroes

I write, how strong and brave they are. That's Darren in a nutshell, not me." In fact, Brandon based many of his male characters off their younger firefighter brother. "I'm going to find a way to get them together." Danica had been so kind to him, ever since the first time he'd called the store about stocking his books. If anyone deserved a happy ending, she did. His hardworking, sacrificial brother deserved a good woman in his life, too.

"You're playing matchmaker in real life now?" Aiden laughed. "Well, if you think Darren's the guy for her, you have your work cut out for you. Have you forgotten his vow of celibacy?"

"No. But I believe in miracles. The four of us prayed for you for years, brother, and look what God did. If He could turn *your* stubborn heart around," he teased, "anything's possible."

Aiden laughed, loud and long. "You know what? I'm going to start praying for you, Bran. There's a perfect woman for you out there, someone who's going to surpass all the fictional women you've created in your mind. And when you meet her, it's going to blow all your romance stories out of the water."

"I appreciate it, but you're gonna have to pray hard, real hard."

It wasn't that Brandon doubted God's power or faithfulness. But it would take something—or someone—extraordinary to surprise him. The truth was he had already met the perfect girl in college. A decade later, and he still couldn't shake his memories of her. Nothing could compare to the romance he'd written for them in his mind.

The one thing he hated about having an overactive imagination? Nothing in real life ever seemed as bright or warm and fuzzy. That's why he'd likely only fall in love in his books ... unless his path crossed again with the first and only woman he'd ever kissed.

Get your copy of *A Sudden Spark* on Amazon.com!

AFTERWORD

This book would not have been possible without the inspiration I got while listening to a local radio station's morning show. One of the deejays shared her random experience of receiving a text message meant for someone else (complete with some internet stalking on her part!) and—*bam!* Abby and Aiden's story was born. :) I decided to make Aiden a former boy band member because I had just watched a reality TV show about the making of a boy band. I grew up loving boy bands (I still have my first New Kids on the Block CD from back in the day) and I love music in general, so it seemed natural to include those elements in this story.

This is also the first time I planned and plotted out an entire series before I wrote it. It was both exciting and challenging for me to figure out all the characters and general storylines ahead of time. As someone who once wished she had an older brother (I'm the oldest of two girls), I thought it'd be interesting to take an inside look at the lives of five brothers. I briefly introduced the other guys to you in this book and am looking forward to sharing each one of their stories in the future.

I hope you enjoyed Abby and Aiden's story! I'd love to hear your feedback (positive or negative), so please leave a review and let me know what you thought. Thank you for reading and giving me a reason to keep writing.

ACKNOWLEDGMENTS

I'd like to thank the following people who blessed me in the making of this book:

My awesome beta readers: Michele Chung, for reminding me to give Aiden closure to his past; Julie Spencer, for encouraging me to make the intro better; and Kristen Iten, for sharing your musical expertise. I appreciate all your detailed, insightful, and constructive feedback. Thank you for taking time out of your busy lives to help me bring Abby and Aiden's story to life.

My fellow authors in the Word War Room Facebook group, for helping me be productive when I needed to crank out lots of words.

My ever-reliable editor, Heather Hayden, for all her hard work in turning my manuscripts into "happy copies".

My online village, Clean Indie Reads, for giving me the practical advice I needed (add more side characters and conflict!) to complete my first novel-length book.

My family, for always supporting me (and reminding me there's more to life than work).

You, dear reader, for believing in me enough to pick up this book and give it a try. Assuming you've read this far, thank you for loving my characters and rooting for them like the real people I know they are! ;)

ABOUT THE AUTHOR

Liwen Y. Ho works as a chauffeur and referee by day (AKA being a stay at home mom) and an author by night. She writes sweet and inspirational contemporary romance infused with heart, humor, and a taste of home (her Asian roots).

In her pre-author life, she received a Master's degree in Marriage and Family Therapy from Western Seminary, and she loves makeovers of all kinds, especially those of the heart and mind. She lives in the San Francisco Bay Area with her techie husband and their two children, and blogs about her adventures as a recovering perfectionist at www.2square2behip.com.

Sign up for Liwen's newsletter to receive an exclusive free book, news about her upcoming releases, giveaways, sneak peeks, and more at: http://eepurl.com/bt2nEL

ALSO BY LIWEN Y. HO

The Spark Brothers Series

A Single Spark

A Sudden Spark

The Sweetest Spark

At First Spark

An Extra Spark

Sage Valley Ranch Series

Falling for the Younger Cowboy

Lawkeepers Series

Lawfully Cherished

Billionaires with Heart Series

At Odds with the Billionaire

Best Friends with the Billionaire

Crushing on the Billionaire

Taking Chances on Love Series

Taking a Chance on the Heartbreaker

Taking a Chance on Mr. Wrong

Taking a Chance on the Enemy

Seasons of Love Series

The More the Merrier

A Spoonful of Spice

Of Buds and Blossoms

On Waves of Wanderlust

Tropical Kiss Series

Tropical Kiss or Miss

Tropical Kiss and Tell

Welcome To Romance Series

Chasing Romance

Romantically Ever After

Holding onto Love in Romance

Non-Series Books

Puppy Dog Tales

The Love Clause

Love's Choice

The Time Rift (co-authored with David H. Ho)

Made in the USA
Monee, IL
14 May 2022

96394960R00094